SPIRIT OF DARKNESS

CLOVERBOOKS

Published By

CL◑VERBOOKS

The moral right of the authors has been asserted in accordance with
the Copyright, Designs and Patents Act 1988

*All characters in this publication are fictitious and any resemblance to real per-
sons, living or dead, is purely coincidental*

A CIP catalogue record for this book is available from the British
Library

ISBN 0 9534290 0 8

Printed and bound in Great Britain by Ashford Colour Press. Gosport, Hants

Clover Books

CBX 2

382-390 Midsummer Boulevard

Central Milton Keynes

MK9 2RG

United Kingdom

Tel: 01908 847500

Contents

The Reivers of Coldshaw Grange

by
Chris Hudson

Chris Hudson

National Serviceman, Marketeer and Business Writer, Chris Hudson wrote his first story whilst soldiering on Cyprus. He has continued to write but was not published before moving to Cumbria with his company director wife and their family dog. At sixty he is compelled to rediscover the complex, violent and supernatural elements existing in the surrounding Fells. His current writing begins when Reiver Families were ruthlessly purged in their Border homelands. This was England's most savage and bloody pacification programme in a region which even today he has discovered, remains untamed and impatiently brooding.

The Reivers of Coldshaw Grange

by

Chris Hudson

Lois Grantham studied her reflection with critical concentration. She had allowed her weight to increase by eighteen pounds, sufficiently over her 'track' weight to maintain her slim figure whilst also pleasing Harold. Her superbly toned limbs, now softly contoured remained elegantly slim. She rested her eyes on her breasts, turning to assess their profile. With the extra weight they had become fuller but still retained their firmness. Smiling with satisfaction she thought of her husband.

At forty nine Harold was not quite twice her age, but that did nothing to reduce his libido. Last night they had made love and again just before full daylight. He had looked at her in the pale light entering the uncurtained windows pulling the duvet below her waist and kissing her breasts in turn. 'The extra weight enhances their allure my darling' he had told her pulling her towards him so she could straddle him. Afterwards they had rested for only a short time before he had to get up for his journey to London. Before leaving he had kissed her dreaming mouth and told her he would be back in two days and rushed downstairs. Remembering his words she now weighed them in her small hands, testing the feel of them.

Taking one last glance she checked her reflection in the full length mirror again before dressing. Her eyes went to the partly open sash window and the gardens beyond. The September air was warm even by her standards, used as she was to southern temperatures. She had wanted Harold to buy Coldshaw Grange from the moment her eyes had recognised its early Georgian magnificence. He had not hesitated. Now that Scotland had devolved it was a perfect location from which to operate his company. They were heavily involved with business in Scotland.

They had moved into the seven bedroom mansion eight weeks earlier. Lois smiled thinking about the plans she had made. In another sixteen months they could celebrate the Millennium. It was so exciting. Hugging herself she looked gleefully around the master bedroom, her agile brain instantly switching to another of her special interests.

The room was not as large as some of the other bedrooms. She had queried this earlier with Stella McBride the new house-keeper. The house had been built for a Crown agent in the early Georgian era, shortly after Bonnie Prince Charlie had been defeated at Culloden Moor in 1746. The land, granted by a grateful King George II, had originally belonged to a Border Family. The house had been destroyed during the years of unrest in that area, but the fifteenth century pele tower had sur-vived, albeit in ruined state. The builders had incorporated the ruin into the fabric of the new house. This, the master bedroom had been one of the tower's three floors. The en suite facilities were, it appeared, a fairly modern refurbishment. Lois made a mental note to talk to Stella again. It was important to her that she learn as much about the history of the house as possible.

She crossed the room and opened the massive oak door notic-ing how her hand spanned its thickness with nothing to spare, yet it opened on its centuries old iron hinges with ease. She tin-gled with pride and satisfaction. She had arrived!

Stella McBride also tingled with emotion. However hers was partly anticipation, partly wonder and partly unease. When the Granthams had bought the Grange she had been the first to apply for the housekeeper's vacancy. At forty she was still attrac-tive, active and well acquainted with the area. She had never married.

When the old house once again changed hands the heightened tension was noticeable in the close knit community. This time close enough to the date to elicit excited comment. Nobody in these parts talked openly about it, but behind closed doors she knew sharp eyes and tongues monitored the situation hourly.

Stella's family had lived in these parts from the seventeenth century, having moved from over the Border into Cumberland after the Scots' King James VI ascended the throne of the new 'Great Britain'. Crowned James I of England in 1603 one of his first deeds was to start the process of cleansing the Reiver Scourge in the borderlands between the two countries. He had paid particular attention to the then infamous Graham Family whom his agents had transported to Ireland where most discovered destitution and death. Stella knew her family and these savage lands' histories in depth. That was why she had been so keen to be appointed housekeeper.

Stella had just finished going through the daily routine with Maggie Tyson the day cook when Lois came into her tidy office.

"Good morning ladies. Please don't let me disturb you. I can wait." Lois's pleasant deep voice never varied. She was always polite.

"There's no need Lois, we've just finished haven't we?" Stella stood up from her desk and nodded to the young cook who pushed between them and left, smiling shyly as she passed her employer.

"I was just making sure you have remembered my brother and sister-in-law are arriving this afternoon Stella. With Harold away for the next couple of days it will be lovely to see Bradley again. Maggie has arranged a light tea and not dinner hasn't she?"

"Yes, as agreed. She'll serve tea at three thirty in the orangery. That leaves you plenty of time to work up an appetite before going out. Have you decided where you're eating?"

"Yes. Harold phoned Chesterton's yesterday. He booked a table for eight o'clock this evening. Brad will get a huge meal and Tina will enjoy the restaurant. I think it's such an elegant place don't you?"

"Well," laughed Stella "I can't say that I frequent the place, but I have eaten there once or twice and always found it marvellous."

Lois had turned while they were talking and walked into the

corridor leading to the main entrance hall. Stella followed her.

"There are one or two things I would like you to do for me Stella...." The housekeeper followed her slim almost delicate employer through to the sitting room making mental notes when Lois pointed out several small things she wanted correcting, determining to speak to the two local cleaning women who came in twice a week. Eventually Lois stopped in the doorway to the dark panelled dining room.

"Stella may I ask you to do me another great favour?"

Stella straightened her shoulders not knowing what to expect from Lois's change in manner.

"Well yes if I can, of course."

"Today is the 17th isn't it? When I was in Carlisle the other day I overheard a conversation in Ottaker's book store. Or part of a conversation anyway. Today's date was mentioned and I am sure the two men were talking about Coldshaw Estate. There isn't another place with the same name is there?"

Lois noticed how unusually pale the housekeeper's face had become.

"Stella are you alright? You look so pale." She rested her neat hand protectively on Stella's arm.

The older woman shook her head quickly pulling herself together.

"I'm sorry Lois I don't know what came over me. I just felt a little strange for a moment that's all. To answer your question," she went on briskly "I am not aware of anywhere else having the same name as this house," she smiled dryly "but what were they saying these two men?"

"Oh I didn't hear much. Just that they mentioned the date '17th September' and the name 'Coldshaw Estate'. It just seemed strange that's all and I wondered if the date meant anything to you."

"There are so many stories, legends or whatever you want to call them. Who can possibly say Lois. I'm sorry I can't be more help. Do you require me for anything else because if not I....."

"No. Thanks Stella. You must have things to do. I'm going out for a while. The weather is so pleasant I think I'll wander round to the walled garden. The herbs smell so lovely in this warmth. Oh, before you go. Would you mind taking some time off to tell me more about the history of Coldshaw and the area? You know so much and it would be nice for me to have a thorough knowledge of the house's background. I'm truly interested in history anyway. Would you.. sometime?"

"It would be my pleasure Lois."

Lois noticed Stella's eyes slid quickly away from her questing look. As she reached down a cotton jacket from the cupboard in the rear hallway Lois thought Stella had not been her usual straight forward self. Something seemed to have upset her normal calm. 'Was she hiding something?' Lois thought as she walked towards the walled garden 'something to do with today's date perhaps. She had seemed edgy when I mentioned those men in Ottakers her brow furrowed as she pondered my question' Lois still had no ideas when she pushed the garden door open and walked into the trapped warmth and the aromatic atmosphere. She dismissed it from her mind. 'Time will tell' she thought enigmatically 'and I must get some flowers for the sitting room before checking Brad and Tina's room.'

Stella heard the car pull up and the doors bang. She was sitting in her room reading a heavy book, its thick, scarred leather cover denoting its age. She listened, resting the book on her lap waiting to hear what happened. The car had driven round to the rear of the house. It was normal for Lois and Mr Grantham to use the rear hall when they had been out in the evening. The front doorway was only used during the daytime and but only when it was considered worthy of the occasion during the evening. She heard the back door bang softly followed by hushed laughter. The clock on the York stone fireplace showed eleven minutes passed eleven. She wondered if they would come straight upstairs or go into the sitting room where the drinks were kept. For several moments she strained her ears listening to catch what she could. She checked the clock again. Twelve minutes passed.

Lois's brother and his wife had been given the Red room on

the front of the house. It was off the same corridor as the master bedroom but further along towards the end.

Stella's suite of rooms was at the back of the house. Opposite the master bedroom but off the stairs leading to the rear corridor. If they had been very quiet she would therefore not necessarily have heard them.

Stella knew she wasn't going to sleep tonight. Putting the heavy tome onto a table she quietly opened the door and went along the short stretch of corridor to the top of the stairs. A single lamp lit the landing where the main staircase divided. The house was quiet. Making little noise on the thick carpet she went downstairs and checked the rooms. Everywhere was in darkness. Careful not to make any sound she checked all the windows in each of the ground floor rooms. It took her a long time to check them all including the back and front doors. She couldn't go into Lois's or her brother's bedrooms but the other five she had checked when they were out at Chesterton's.

Silently she returned to her rooms. It was a warm night. She hoped without much confidence that neither Lois nor the others had opened their bedroom windows to let in the night's cool breeze.

Still fully clothed Stella settled into the deep old armchair and picked up the heavy book and started reading. The mantle clock read two minutes to midnight,

Startled by the loudness of the scream Stella jerked upright, the book falling off her lap where it had rested when she had drifted off.

The room was in complete darkness. Still disorientated her brain puzzled why this should be as she reached for the light switch. Nothing! She tried it several times but still nothing. Groping through the pitch dark she berated herself for not having foreseen this likelihood. Her fingers found the cupboard where she kept a torch for emergencies. Switching it on she was astounded when that too failed to work.

She started to gasp in panic when the next scream, longer and more demented echoed through the house. Stella pushed both hands over her ears in a useless effort to keep the terror from invading her brain. Another scream, more terrible and insistent than the last reached her. Disabled by the darkness she struggled to the door. Despite having become used to the layout over the past ten weeks since she had moved in to prepare the house for the new owners, her fear had robbed her of all rational thought and for a moment she could not remember which way she had to go.

Feeling along the wall with her hands she stumbled along the short corridor onto the stair. The screams coming from across the central landing were now continuous. Cold sweat poured down her back, soaking her.

Stumbling down the short arm of the stairs she fumbled her way on all fours up the opposite flight. When she reached the top she knew she had to turn left to reach the master bedroom door. As she stood upright off her knees to reach for the wall, a darker patch bumped into her. Terrified, her heart pounding painfully she added her scream to the terrified noises escaping through the thick oak door and nearly fell.

"For God's sake is that you Stella?"

She recognised the voice of Bradley Armitage, Lois's brother.

"Yes it's me." She gulped. A stillness fell on the house. Eerie in its abruptness.

"What the hell's going on Stella? Is that Lois making that terrible noise? Can't you do something? Why have the lights gone out?" He sounded stricken.

"I don't know any more than you. Quick. Come with me." She fumbled for his arm and pulled him towards the bedroom door. "help me open this door."

Stella turned the big iron ring and pushed just as Lois started screaming again. Now she could see tiny chinks of orange light flickering through the cracks in the ancient door. The door refused to budge.

"Help me Brad!" She screamed helplessly. "Help me!"

She felt him move alongside her, push her hand away from the iron handle and grunt with the effort of heaving against the door. Even with his help the door remained firmly shut.

Stella crouched huddled against the smooth door. She could smell fumes. Tiny tendrils of smoke eddied around the door's edges.

"Oh God there's a fire in there." She cried out desperately.

Despite their combined efforts they failed to move the door. Stella noticed Lois's screams had now dropped to a lower pitch. With tears stinging her face she listened to the pitiful pleas. With horror she realised she could hear a deep rumbling sound in the gaps between Lois's shrieks of terror. She pressed her ear to the door, her heart frozen with understanding. The noises were the sounds of men's raucous laughter. The thick stone walls and heavy oak door muffled much of the sound, but as she listened she became surer of what she heard. Her ears straining, she tried to make sense of the weak female cries. Her brain unscrambled the unintelligible sounds. Stella heard the agonised despair in Lois's voice as she pleaded with her tormentors. Suddenly she heard the rumble of deep voices raised in unison, followed by another short eerie silence. Stella held her breath. When the blood curdling scream shattered the nerve jangling silence she reeled from the door and fell writhing helplessly onto the landing carpet. A deathly silence filled the house.

The examining judge bowed to the standing court officials, swiftly assuring himself the public gallery had been kept empty, and sat down.

"Mr Hardern. This court of enquiry is minded to accept your plea on behalf of the Police prosecution to hear the evidence in camera. Will you please proceed."

"Thank you your Honour. I have two witnesses to call. My first witness is a medical expert. I call Professor Gerrardson."

The barrister watched as the tall, spare professor was sworn in and then went through the preamble of ascertaining his identity and qualifications. Satisfied he asked the pathologist to give a detailed account of Mrs Lois Grantham's injuries.

The professor gave his account, reading from his notes when necessary but in the main speaking from memory in his low educated voice. When he had finished he looked at the judge and coughed.

"Yes Professor. You wish to add something?"

"Your Honour I wish to say that in all my very considerable experience I have never found it necessary to carry out such an extraordinary autopsy. This case is most perplexing. Whilst I am certain that the deceased was subjected to a prolonged and vicious attack I am astounded by the ferocity and strength of these attacks. I just wanted to make this clear to the Court."

"Yes thank you Professor, the court is grateful. Before you stand down would you please clarify one thing for me. You say in your written statement that the deceased was subjected to multiple rape. Can you say how many times?"

"Not with certainty your Honour. The DNA samples taken from the deceased body totalled thirteen. This would mean the deceased had been raped by thirteen different men. However on the evidence of the injuries......internal not external your Honour...I would not be surprised if that number was fifty percent higher."

"Good God." The judge was visibly discomfited. He nodded his head, dismissing the professor.

"Now Mr Hardern may we go on. This is a most harrowing business. The sooner we get on the sooner we will finish."

The barrister rose and addressed the bench. "If it pleases the Court may I ask that the second witness, in view of this most unusual case and in order to save the Court's time, be allowed to give her evidence and then be cross examined should the Court so wish?"

"I see no reason why that should not be possible Mr Hardern. Yes you may go ahead."

"Thank you your Honour. I call Miss Stella McBride."

The barrister watched as Stella McBride stepped into the box and was sworn in by the Clerk.

"Miss McBride will you please tell us what happened at the house known as 'Coldshaw Grange,' the present home of Mr Harold Grantham and the late Mrs Lois Grantham."

Stella began by telling the court of the day's happenings on September 17th. She went into graphic detail right up to the time when Lois screamed for the last time.

When she had finished, she stood palely waiting. The judge

looked at Hardern but decided to say nothing.

"Miss McBride," the barrister rose and asked heavily "you made a statement to Chief Inspector Rawlings? Will you please now tell this court what you said in that statement."

Before she could start the barrister turned to the judge and said levely "Your copy number A5 your Honour."

The judge nodded, lifting a sheaf of papers to indicate he had it.

Stella McBride began. "Your honour, my family line goes back into the late 16th century. A distant relative on my mother's side was the leader and a magistrate in the Border counties between England and Scotland. His name was Kerr. He it was in 1610, who led a hot trod which captured 'Black Peg' Graham."

"Let me stop you there Miss McBride," interrupted the judge "what is a hot trod?"

"It was a right granted by the Authorities in the 17th century, for men to pursue, capture and try thieves or Reivers as they were called then, within six days of a robbery your Honour"

The judge nodded his thanks ."And who was 'Black Peg' Graham?"

"He was a notorious murderer. A member of one of the infamous Reiver Families. In this case a Graham."

She looked up at the judge to see if he was satisfied. He nodded.

"When the hot trod cornered the gang on their way back from a raid into Eskdale, they had been enraged and fought a bitter battle. The Reivers having killed the men folk defending their home on a small but wealthy farmstead, had then viciously raped all the women they could lay their hands on. They were so bestial in their lust that very few survived their torment, and those survivors did not include one single young women, all of whom had been unable to withstand their ordeal. It had been the raiders particular pleasure to cut off the women's breasts when they had no further use for them."

There were thirteen Reivers. All but 'Black Peg' Graham and three others were killed in the fight. My forebear being a magistrate, held a field court of justice. Graham and his three men were sentenced to be summarily hanged."

"According to contemporary records, 'Black Peg' Graham was

a huge man. Well set up. Despite his serious wounds it took five men to hold him. When they hanged him, although the rope was of mature hemp it stretched so much under his weight, even though he had been standing on his horse's saddle, that his boots were barely a hand's span off the ground by the time he kicked his last."

"However before the hot trod put the rope around his neck, 'Black Peg' swore an oath." Stella read from a notepad, "Ony English mon bides in ane's aught thi' batch o' diels dizzen wi' nick the guid-wife's breasties til' she screigh. I man swear."

Stella looked up at the judge, saw his confusion as she had expected and quickly explained "Of course, language has changed considerably since the seventeenth century but what this means in modern English is "Any English man who resides in my property, this gang of the devil's dozen...or sometimes thirteen...will severe the lady of the house's breasts until she screams. I am forsworn."

A sudden appalled silence fell over the courtroom. Stella looked first at the judge then at the barrister. Hardern seeing her confusion stood up.

"Was that all Miss McBride? Or do you have something more to say? If so please tell the court."

"Well yes, there is more. When Mr Armitage helped me to try to open the door to Mrs Grantham's bedroom, I distinctly heard the rumble of men's voices from the other side. When shortly after we heard that last terrible screaming, the light on the landing suddenly came back on. Mr Armitage switched all the other lights on and we found we were then able to get into the bedroom. Mrs Grantham was lying on the bed. It is a very large four poster bed. She was spread across it, in the middle of the blood which had sprayed from the terrible wounds on her body."

Stella McBride stumbled over the next words. The judge intervened.

"Are you capable of continuing Miss McBride? Would you prefer me to call a recess for half an hour perhaps?"

Stella raised her face, tears glittering on the lashes. "Thank you your Honour but I would prefer to carry on now that I have got this far. There's not a lot more.....it was a terrifying sight. We were stunned for a while. Both of us had at first suspected she had been trapped in a fire because we had smelt smoke coming under the door when we tried to open it. And I had seen orange flickering lights through some of the small cracks in the wood. Anyway Mrs Grantham was clearly dying. Her wounds must have made it very painful to breathe, but she did speak before she died. Mr Armitage heard her too. She had difficulty speaking but I heard her plainly. She said 'tell.. Harold... to. go.. away... then... they... will... let.. me go.' Then she died."

"There is one final thing I would say your Honour. 'Black Peg' Graham and the other Reivers were hanged on the 17th September 1610. It may have been a co-incidence but nobody around here who knows anything about its past believes it was your Honour. There's been much evil in these parts and much of it may not be far away even today. You'll not find any evidence that Mrs Grantham was murdered by anyone from this side of Hell....of that I'm certain. The house alarm was set so no mortal persons broke in that night. But there is reason to believe that 'Black Peg Graham' kept his oath. The pele tower at Coldshaw had been the Graham's property. I hope Mr Grantham will now go away. He was the first Englishman to live in the big house. If he leaves...then Lois will find peace."

©Chris Hudson

Cherry Pie

by
Peter Mottley

Peter Mottley

Peter graduated at the University of Sheffield in Philosophy and English before becoming a professional actor, then scriptwriter. Several of his plays have been produced professionally, including AFTER AGINCOURT, THE LAST WILL & TESTAMENT OF POPSY PETAL, BEFORE NELL and A MATTER OF ETIQUETTE.

AFTER AGINCOURT was also produced on Radio 3, with Bob Hoskins. Other plays on the amateur circuit include LIZ and DEAD TROUBLE.

He has had one novel published, THE SEX BAR, and has completed another.

Cherry Pie

by

Peter Mottley

"**W**hat the hell...?"

We'd all three of us arrived back on the forecourt at the same time. Me and Colin from the Gents, Mo from the service station shop where she'd been paying for the petrol.

"Bloody cheek!" I said.

There was this man, total stranger, sitting in the passenger seat.

Colin was more direct. Well, he's Australian. He would be. He pulled open the door and jerked his thumb over his shoulder. "You, mate," he said. "Out!"

"I'm awfully sorry," the man said. Nicely spoken, suit and tie, briefcase. "I was hoping you might be able to give me a lift. You see, my own car -"

"Out!" Colin said.

"Even if you want a lift," I said, "you don't just push into someone else's car. I mean..."

"Come on, you guys," said Mo. "It's nearly one o'clock in the morning, and it's pissing down with rain. Where's the harm?" She's Australian, too. Just as direct as her brother, but less aggressive. That's probably why I married her. "What happened to your own car?" She said to the passenger.

He shrugged in a slightly embarrassed way. "Puncture. And I...er...I've never had to change a wheel before. So I managed to get it this far, and...well, they're going to sort it out for me tomorrow. In the meantime, I need a lift. I'd be awfully grateful

27

if...well..." He paused for a moment, then started to get out of the car. "I'm sorry..."

"It's OK," said Mo. "If it's not too far out of our way, we'd be happy to drop you off. We're going home to Oxford." She turned to me. "That OK, Pom?" It's a nickname I picked up in Oz when I was working there with Colin. That's how I met Mo in the first place.

I shrugged. "Suppose so."

"That would be perfect," he said.

So me and Colin piled into the back, and Mo set off.

"Rescued everything I needed to rescue," he said, tapping his briefcase. He held up his right hand. He was holding a clear plastic wallet with a few folded documents in it. "Including the bits you tend to forget. You know, the bits you put into the pocket in the driver's visor." He laughed self-depracatingly. "You always forget the important bits."

Me and Colin weren't saying anything. Still a bit pissed off. But Mo had said she was giving him a lift, and Mo was driving that night, so it was nothing to do with us.

Until he opened his briefcase and got out this packet of cherry pies. Well, not *actually* cherry pies. A sort of Bakewell tart with a cherry on the top. But he said "Would anyone like a cherry pie?"

Nobody said a word.

"Last one," he said. "I ate the other three while I was waiting."

Still nobody said a word.

He held the pie out to Mo. "*You* like cherry pies," he said. "Go on, have a bite."

She ignored him.

"Go on," he said, "have a bite." It was weird. A total stranger, yet he'd suddenly become all playful. He was waving the cake under Mo's nose, teasing her, goading her. "You *love* cherry pie... Think of all the things we could do with a cherry pie...! Go on, have a nibble." Now there were starting to be sexy undertones.

I was just about to tell him to leave it out, when Mo swiped his arm away from her face. "I don't want a sodding cherry pie!"

The car wobbled briefly, brushed the kerb, swung into the middle of the road, then straightened.

"Mo! Stop the car!" Colin had decided to take charge.

She pulled over to the side, put her hazard lights on and waited.

Colin leaned forward and put his head between her and the passenger. "Now, look," he said. "We won't make you get out, because it's a bloody awful night. But from now until we get where we're going, keep your hands in your lap and your mouth shut. Got it?"

He nodded. "Sorry," he muttered.

Colin leaned back in his seat again. "You're a bloody menace," he said. "OK, Mo." She slipped it into gear, and we moved off.

We'd only gone a couple of hundred yards when he leaned forward, peered through the beating windscreen wipers, and said "This is it." We were just coming up to a roundabout, one of those roundabouts that don't seem to have been put there for any particular purpose. No houses, no pub, not even a service station. Just a couple of tiny unlit roads that didn't look as if they went anywhere.

"You sure?" Mo said. "Don't mind Colin. I'll take you to your door if it's not too far away. You don't want to be walking in this weather."

"Honestly, this is it," he said. "Anywhere on the roundabout."

Mo pulled over. He opened the door, got out, then leaned his head back in. "Thanks ever so much," he said. "Sorry to have bothered you." He shut the door and stood there, the rain flattening his hair and soaking into his suit.

Mo waited a few seconds to see if he wanted to change his mind. But he just stood there, so she moved off. When we reached the other side of the roundabout, I turned round to see which of the two minor roads he took, but he was still standing there, looking after us, getting drenched.

"Bloody menace," Colin muttered. Nobody else said anything at all for the rest of the journey.

We were supposed to be going to Stonehenge the next day.

Colin was over for three weeks, and he was very keen on ancient monuments. Well, he and Mo are part Abo, and they don't have a great deal of ancient monuments of their own back home.

Me and Colin were in the kitchen finishing off our coffee when Mo came in. "You'll never guess what that silly bugger last night has done," she said, waving a clear plastic wallet at us. "Left his driving licence on the seat."

Colin took it from her and pulled out the contents. "And his insurance certificate."

"*And*," said Mo, "that bloody cherry pie!" We all laughed. This morning it was funny.

"Who gets to eat it?" I said. "Do we draw lots?"

"It's in the bin," said Mo.

"Safest place for it," said Colin, and we all laughed again.

I took the driving licence off Colin, and looked at the address. Frank Jefferson. "Well, he doesn't live anywhere near the place we dropped him off. According to this, he lives in the middle of Oxford."

"Probably got a sheila on the side. The sort that goes for dripping wet donks in the middle of the night."

Mo peered over my shoulder. "What do you reckon, Pom?" She said. "Drop it in on him when we go out? We virtually have to pass the end of his road on the way through."

"Suits me. As long as he doesn't invite us in for tea and cherry pie." Pretty pathetic, but we all found it hilarious.

Just the sort of house I would have expected. Modest semi, neat lawn at the front, flowerbed under the bay window. Mo kept the engine running while I nipped out, walked up the brick-laid path, and rang the bell. A face stirred briefly through the bottle-glass window, then the heavy wooden door opened.

Middle-aged woman, a few years older than I would have expected. She looked at me oddly. Normally, when a perfect stranger knocks on your door you look at him suspiciously, or welcomingly, or at least questioningly. She just looked at me like she was expecting me.

"Mrs Jefferson?" I said.

"You've brought back his driving licence." It wasn't a question.

"Er, yes." I put my hand up to my shirt pocket. Not there. Hip pocket? Not there, either. I was starting to feel a bit foolish.

Mo wound the window down and called out from the car. "You all right, Pom?"

"Er, yes... Er, did I give Mr Jefferson's driving licence to you?"

"It's in your shirt pocket."

I turned to Mrs Jefferson. "Sorry about this. I must have dropped it in the car. Won't be a moment." I turned to go, but she stopped me.

"I think you'd better come in," she said. "I think you're owed an explanation." I looked over my shoulder at the car. "All of you," she said.

She didn't offer us tea or anything. Just told us the story, straight.

"Six years ago, my husband got a puncture on his way home from work. To be honest, I wasn't expecting him home that night. He was supposed to be at a conference in Manchester. He managed to get as far as a garage on the A34."

Me and Mo and Colin looked at each other. We'd picked him up on the A34.

"He begged a lift from a young woman. Afterwards, she said she'd never seen him before, but..." But she didn't seem convinced. She shrugged. "She lost control of her car on a roundabout, and crashed it."

I could feel the hairs on the back of my neck prickling. Too many coincidences

"The driver's side had an airbag. The passenger side didn't." She stood up. We stood up with her. The interview was over.

"The police found his driving licence in the car when they towed it away." When she looked at us, there was real pain in her eyes.

"It was in the back seat. The *back* seat, do you see? Why should his things be in the back seat when he was in the front seat?"

Mo was as shaken as I was. "I found it on the back seat. I hadn't thought of that..."

"How did you know I'd come to..." I tailed off. I didn't really want to know the answer.

She looked away. The pain had turned to weariness again. "Every year, on this day, someone comes to return his driving licence. Perhaps it's his way of asking me to forgive him."

Again, I felt in my pockets for it, but she stopped me. "You won't find it," she said. "It's gone." She walked into the passageway and opened the front door for us. "It's gone now until next year."

As we left, all I could think of to say was something incredibly stupid. Confused, I suppose, or shaken. Or both. "There was a cherry pie as well," I said.

She nodded. "Yes. There's always a cherry pie."

Nobody said anything till we got back to the main road. Then Mo turned left instead of right.

"What about Stonehenge?" Colin asked her.

"Bugger Stonehenge - there's a cherry pie in my bin with a jinx on it! I'm not having it in the house. We're going home."

In the end, she put newspaper on the floor and tipped the bin out on it. We all three of us sifted through it, bit by bit.

But there was no sign of the cherry pie.

©Peter Mottley

Macau Interlude

by
Charles Marshall

Charles Marshall

Charles is forty six years old but looks, he insists, considerably younger, in a rugged, intense way. His interest in the darker side stems mainly from witnessing people do unpleasant things to one another whilst he was in the army serving in Northern Ireland and latterly during twenty years in the Royal Hong Kong Police whence he took early retirement to pursue a life of bucolic pleasure in Scotland. The exchange rate however wounded his pension mortally and he took to writing about thinly disguised incidents and acquaintances in an effort to maintain the hire purchase payments on his Rolls Royce.

Macau Interlude

by

Charles Marshall

The table went quiet as the croupier closed the betting. He spun the roulette wheel counter-clockwise with one hand and rolled the steel ball into the spinning numbers with the other. As it slowed , the ball dipped towards the 38 numbered recesses on the wheel and it jumped skittishly before settling. "Number two, red", announced the croupier. There was a collective sigh, the sound of losers and the croupier deftly raked the chips towards the bank.

All except one. Jerry Lai had bet on the red four consecutive times and his original stake of $1,000 had become $16,000. It was an unusual run but not of any import: the table's margin was sufficient to cover many times that. In the seedy world of the Macau casinos, the money wagered and largely lost is out of all proportion to the tacky surroundings. Jerry smiled. Turning to his left, he saw a young woman standing behind him. She was unusual, given that unattached women in casinos were either in raucous groups of Hong Kong housewives out for a night away from their menfolk or hollow eyed compulsive gamblers. If drink was the chief vice of westerners, it was gambling for the Chinese. That and drugs, the latter of which was of course common to both.

She was expensively dressed and extremely attractive, her hair cut in such a way as to frame her face and enhance further a flawless complexion and brown, deep set eyes. Jerry's lingering glance took in the fact that she was a mature woman, possibly in her early thirties. Skillfully applied makeup could not altogether disguise the lines around her eyes and her lips had the fullness of experience. Was she also vaguely familiar? She returned his glance coolly but with a hint of... what? invitation? interest? She spoke. "Lucky in gambling, unlucky in life. That's what the gweilo say, isn't it?"

Jerry smiled. He was 35 and lived in one of the three Hong Kong apartments he owned in the expensive South Bay area. His family fortune had been founded a generation ago in still a profitable clothing factory in China which Jerry had inherited as the only son. The two daughters had been allocated suitable husbands and small dowries. But the bulk of Jerry's vast fortune came from a third share of another Macau casino which he had bought with the proceeds from his own holding in the family business. His conservative brothers had been delighted to buy out their flamboyant younger brother and they continued to make money, steadily and unobtrusively. Jerry preferred the casinos: there was power in controlling the greed of others, power which for Jerry, far outweighed any pleasure in gambling itself.

"Depends on the gambler", he smiled. He knew the type of woman she was: a gambling groupie. Not exactly a prostitute but seduced by the power of people like himself who could make money appear, seemingly at will. In Jerry's experience, such women got a big buzz out of high rollers like himself.

"See those chips?" She nodded. "Why don't you take them over to the desk, cash them and wait for me for a couple of minutes." He shrugged. "It,s a small amount but enough for a little fun." She looked at him appraisingly and smiled. There was anticipation in the smile, he decided.

"Why not? I've nothing else on tonight. See you in a couple of minutes. My name's Su-lin, by the way."

"Jerry. Jerry Lai," he replied, passing a $500 chip to the croupier before he left the table. Such tips were 'expected' and whilst Lai was protected by virtue of his place in the casino fraternity, it was a courtesy he liked to extend. Others less elevated than himself would probably receive a powerful and unsubtle hint that table gratuities were expected.. Macau, he reflected, could be a dangerous place but not to those in the ruling elite. . Lai went to the lavatory, relieved himself and checked his appearance briefly. Good living was taking its toll but he still cut a well-tailored figure and wealth could hide any number of physical shortcomings. His appearance was a little flashy for some tastes, but what the hell did he care? Like many of the newly rich, he liked to display it.

The woman smiled as he approached. She was looking sleek and glamorous, her long dress tight around the bodice and hips and she was carrying an overnight bag. He raised an eyebrow.

"I couldn't leave it here." She shrugged. "Anyway, I thought you wanted some fun."

"Absolutely. I see you believe in appearances, as well," he nodded at her wedding ring. She smiled again.

"Oh yes, precautions are most important, don't you think?" She spoke slowly, picking her words with care. Lai understood. A woman such as her wouldn't want to take chances on picking up HIV or anything else. Her lifestyle dictated she slept with many men and unnecessary risks were to be avoided. That was all right with Lai. He genuinely liked women but he did not greatly respect them. After all, if they were truly worthy of respect, why were they willing to allow themselves to be violated so cheaply? Lai had an equitable but distant relationship with his own wife, who he viewed as a necessary social accoutrement and potential mother of his children. If she failed to fulfil either task satisfactorily she would, of course, have to go.

Jerry Lai was a careful man, too careful to return to his own hotel. Whilst he was not overly concerned about word getting back to his wife of a little extra-curricular activity, he did not really need the hassle. If an extra two thousand bucks would keep his little secret, so be it. Anyway, there was always the possibility of his escort nosing about his room when he wasn't looking and, well, blackmail could be intensely embarrassing as well as expensive.

"Shall we go?" Asked Lai, offering his arm. She took it in a cool, firm grasp, her fingertips teasing gently at the nerves in the inner biceps.

"Of course, your place or mine."

"Neither. I haven't been to the Hyatt on Taipa for at least two years. I'd like to see it again (and they won't remember me there, either, he added to himself).

"Sounds good. Do you have a car?"

"Afraid not. Have to be a taxi." She shrugged

"Its not too far and the Hyatt sounds fine. What shall we do there?" She smiled up at him in false innocence.

Lai grinned and felt his body respond. It was going to be worth a few thousand was tonight. He hailed one of the many scruffy and suitably anonymous Macau taxis, which barged through the normally chaotic Macau traffic before ascending the smooth dual carriageway of the new Taipa bridge, a two kilometre showpiece primarily designed to service the new airport on Taipa Island.

At night, from the bridge, Macau regains some of the mystique which fifteen years of virtually uncontrolled development has robbed it. The stark skeletons of artless half constructed buildings are mercifully hidden and you can still pick out the beautifully restored Belavista Hotel. Even the Lisboa Hotel and Casino complex, by day amongst the ugliest buildings to be seen anywhere, look almost acceptable at night.

The trip took little more than ten minutes, during which time Su-lin did not object as Lai stroked her thigh lasciviously, fingers lingering as he moved his hand upwards and inwards. Jerry withdrew his hand as the taxi drew up to the Hyatt, otherwise known as the Taipa Island Resort. It was less garish than the Lisboa and in considerably better taste. Jerry was careful not to tip the driver too much. Firstly it was a waste of money and secondly drivers tended to remember the givers of large tips. It was all part of being careful. As Lai told his wife constantly, it might cost a little to be careful but it invariably cost a great deal more being careless.

The couple walked into the brightly lit lobby. Su-lin reached into her bag for a pair of sunglasses.

"I'm a night bird, " she laughed "and the bright lights get to me. It's different in the casino." It was. There, the lighting was strategic, only the 'bear pits' being brilliantly lit, partly to attract the punters and partly to allow plenty of light for the hidden cameras to pick up any sharp practice on the part of the public or the croupiers. Together, they approached the desk, for all the world like any other wealthy Hong Kong couple, tired at the end of a long evening. The front desk manager noticed but did not mention the fact that they had only one small bag between them. The man's gold Amex card was sufficient proof of his bona fides for the hotel.

Lai waved away the offer of bellboy assistance, collected his key (actually a plastic coded card) and nodded to the clerk, who smiled back brightly and emptily, wishing them both a pleasant evening. In the lift, Su-lin kept her dark glasses on but moved closer to Lai and blatantly cupped her elegant hand around his groin, squeezing gently.

"Aah, Christ that's good", he groaned, his penis hardening against her skillful touch. Cunningly, Su-lin had disguised her move from the lift camera by hefting her bag into the lens's field of vision and she whispered this to Jerry.

"You know, you and I have a lot in common: I appreciate discretion and care and I'm not afraid to pay for it."

Su-lin nodded. "I think we understand each other, Jerry." She paused. The lift reached the eight floor and as they walked into the heavily carpeted corridor. "Would you be talking about a permanent position or just something temporary?"

Lai had done this before. Concubinage had a long history in China and it was fairly common practice for wealthy Hong Kong men to maintain mistresses. Of course, the risk was lessened if such commodities were lodged away from home. Kwantung province was popular and cheap but Macau had its advantages, being a little more sophisticated than the chaotic sprawl of Shum Chun city, just across the Sino-Hong Kong border. Lai's last mistress had been in Shum Chun but she had been greedy and Lai was far from the only man who crossed the threshold into her flat, which Lai paid for. He had been incensed when he found out and felt totally justified in having the woman seriously beaten up and thrown out on the street, without her belongings. The rule of law and social security were not common currency in Shum Chun and Lai rightly expected no comeback for his action. He had been careful to pay the correct people, after all.

He shrugged. "Let's discuss it later. After all, we need to get to know each other, if we're to have a long term relationship." The unspoken implication was of course, was she prepared to indulge Lai in whatever sexual peccadilloes he liked. He thought she would be.

Their room was standard upper end tourist hotel. Good quality prints (screwed to rather than hung on the wall), king-sized double bed, comfortable chairs, en suite bath and shower and remote -controlled TV with video channel. Lai knew the pay by view channel would also include adult films. He closed and bolted the door.

Turning, he caught his breath as he saw Su-lin. She slipped the dress off her shoulders and the soft material hissed sensuously down the length of her body, piling in a small, shiny heap on the carpet. Her body was classic, with small, firm breasts, untouched by childbearing. She ran her hands down firm, long thighs and stepped out of her high-heeled shoes towards him.

He grabbed greedily, squeezing her left breast in one hand, pulling her towards him with the other. She pulled away, gently.

"I know you're in a hurry but we've got all night so what's the rush. If this is going to be a relationship, I want to be treated right so why don't you run me a bath while I order the champagne?"

Lai forced himself to relax. He was desperate for sex but felt that he should match the woman's level of control. He breathed deeply. "Okay, but you do the bath and I'll order." He touched her breast again, this time more gently. "Since we're celebrating, we'll make it Krug."

She nodded slowly and headed into the bathroom. It was working, she thought.

The water pressure was high and she heard his voice on the telephone above the roar of the taps. Timing was important. Lai returned to the bathroom. He too had undressed. Su-lin had wrapped herself in a towel and handed Lai one of the bathrobes. Bereft of his expensive clothes, he was not impressive. He was already running to fat and his limbs were skinny, with the unhealthy pallor of one who spends most of his time indoors.

"You don't want to greet room service with that on display" she laughed," pointing at his still semi-erect penis. "Once the champagne arrives, its your turn in the bath and when you come out, I'll be ready."

"All right, but a shower is all I'll be needing." His expression was an unattractive mixture of lust and greed. Rather like a tycoon faced with the chance to ruin a competitor, she thought, in good Hong Kong fashion.

Su-lin luxuriated briefly in the hot, scented water, whilst Lai donned the bathrobe she had given him and he walked back to the bedroom, stopping at the mini bar to help himself to a Black Label miniature. He added ice and moved to the window, inspecting Su-lin's case as he did so. It was locked, with two four digit combination locks. She was careful, he thought.

A knock on the door interrupted his musing. A courteous waiter wheeled in a trolley covered with a linen tablecloth of dazzling brilliance. An ice bucket, beaded with water droplets, stood in the centre, containing a dark bottle which leaned at a jaunty angle. Two tulip glasses flanked the bucket, chess pawns guarding a bacchanalian king. There were also two plates each with its small pot of caviar. A larger plate, topped with a napkin, contained a small stack of blinis. Finger bowls, each with a floating orchid petal, completed a picture of wealth and elegance.

"Shall I open the champagne sir?"

"No, I'll do it later. That's all. Now get out." He signed the bill and the waiter smilingly bade him good night on the way out, thinking dark thoughts about rude bastards with far more money than manners. He hoped the sod would get the pox or worse from that woman he had brought up with him. The waiter had been in the business quite long enough to spot costly one night stands. And not even a tip. He stalked off down the corridor.

Su-lin heard the door close and let the water out of the bath. Drying herself, she dropped the towel and walked back to the bedroom, naked.

Lai turned. "You are really something, you know that?"

She nodded. "Now, your turn in the shower, while I get ready."

"You look pretty much ready to me."

"Oh, just a few finishing touches. Two minutes. No more." She turned away, slowly, letting him catch her marvellous profile.

"Two minutes. Right!" He hurried to the bathroom.

Su-lin quickly dialled the combination locks and opened her case. first, she pulled out a long pair of black satin gloves and drew them on, carefully. She then put two bottles of scent on the side table and placed a few drops of Chanel behind her ears, before closing and locking her case. Moving quickly, she went to the trolley and picked the champagne from the ice bucket. Twisting off the wire with gloves on was tricky but she managed it.

Lai heard the cork pop from inside the shower and turned the water off, reaching for a towel. He brushed his teeth and took a final look in the mirror, seeing a rather different image to that noted by Su-lin. He dropped the towel on the floor (what are servants for, anyway?) and closed the door behind him.

Su-lin was standing in the middle of the floor, smiling broadly, her lips lifted. She looked almost triumphant, he thought, taking in the long, sexy gloves and otherwise complete nudity. Triumphant and incredibly sexy.

"Wow," was all he said.

She stood close to him and handed him a glass. "Here you are Jerry, and here's to us. Yum Sing!" Throwing back a glass of champagne that expensive in a single gulp might have offended a purist but Jerry was no purist and he followed suit, joining in the game. She refilled the glasses

She had more games. "Come on, sit on the bed, while we watch ten minutes of the adult channel." She looked at him mischievously and Jerry, buoyed by the champagne and the prospect of a memorable night, was happy to indulge her. Su-lin flicked through the remote channels before arriving at the predictable scenes of grainy, writhing bodies, complete with artificially loud sound track. In spite of himself, Jerry felt drowsy. She leant towards him, gloved fingers tracing from his nipples down slowly to his groin. Even as he felt the blood race back to his groin, a wave of sleepiness washed over him, his eyes closed and his breathing became deep and regular.

Su-lin waited another ten minutes. She then squeezed his testicle gently, then harder. No reaction. She got up briskly from the bed and opened her suitcase again. She took out a roll of surgical tape, cheap plastic paper cutter, the ubiquitous two dollar variety with extremely sharp snap-off blades, a black photograph wallet, a disposable syringe, a quarter full of clear liquid and lastly a coil of thick braided nylon cord. She returned the two scent bottles to the case. The one containing Chanel was practically full, the other half empty. It did not smell of Chanel.

She pulled on the spare bathrobe and set to work. Pulling the unconscious Lai down the bed, she arranged his limbs in spread eagle form. Then she cut four ten foot lengths of cord and tied one to each wrist and ankle, leading the tail of each binding below the bed and securing it to the leg. She cut one more length from the coil, doubled it around Lai's flabby waist then led one end under the bed, before attaching it to the other end. She didn't really think it was necessary but precautions never did any harm. Except to you, she thought, looking at the unconscious body with distaste.

Su-lin checked Lai's breathing and sat down on the opposite side of the trolley, watching him whilst she finished the caviar and blinis and helped herself to another glass of Bollinger. It really was very good, she thought. she would try it again sometime. She took her time eating and it was twenty minutes before she stood up and pushed the trolley to the corner of the room. Then, still wearing her gloves, she went through Lai's suit. In his wallet, she found ten one thousand dollar notes and smaller denominations making up twelve thousand in all. She removed the money, his gold cufflinks and gold Rolex watch, placing them all carefully in her case. From his belt, she unclipped his pager and mobile phone, switched them off and placed them in her case as well. Finished, she moved her chair round and watched the last hour of a rather tedious comedy starring Steve Martin. She stood up, stretched and checked her watch. It was 1.30 A.M. Time for sleep.

Su-lin checked Lai. His pulse was slow but strong, commensurate with his drugged state. His eyeballs were turned up and she had little doubt he would sleep for the next three hours. Satisfied he was not going to choke on his tongue, she took a pillow from the bed and lay down on the floor. She set her watch alarm for four a.m., rolled onto her side and fell asleep. It had been a long, tiring day and night.

Two and a half hours later, her watch beeped insistently and she woke, stiff from the hard floor. She went into the bathroom, washed briefly and returned to the bedroom. Lai was not yet stirring but his sleep pattern was changing. He was obviously in some unconscious discomfort from his bound wrists and ankles. Hands and feet were both puffy and tinged with blue. She checked the bonds, which were still tight. She picked up the syringe and located the vein in the crook of his elbow. Skillfully inserting the needle, she slowly expelled the contents. He twitched as she did so but relaxed immediately. It would not take long. Carefully capping the syringe, she replaced it in her case and picked up the paper cutter.

The stimulant coursed rapidly through Lai's veins and within two minutes he was stirring. His eyes half - opened, closed then opened wide. She held the cutter so close he could barely focus on it.

"Don't say a word and most importantly, don't shout. If you do so, I will cut your throat. Do you understand?" He nodded.

"Now, I want you to understand that you cannot move and you cannot escape. So try. As hard as you can"

"You fu...." she drew the blade quickly across his throat and Lai felt a brief burning sensation. Su-lin took a make up mirror from the side table and held it to his face. He swallowed as he saw the blood bead across his throat.

"It's not a deep cut but I wanted to show you how easy it is. Now, speak only when I tell you to and do what you're told. Okay?" He nodded, eyes wide.

"Now, struggle." Lai pulled but the pain in his wrists and ankles and the stretched out nature of his limbs meant he was incapable of exerting any pressure. "All right, Jerry," she emphasised his name.

"Now, its time for a bedtime story and this one has pictures." She laughed softly, without mirth. "But first, a question: why do you think you're here and what do you think I want? Answer, but keep your voice down."

"Money?" He whispered. "Look, take my wallet and I'll give you my PIN number for my cash card - you can get another ten thousand on that. Its 2424." She nodded.

"Lucky number eh? twice times four equals eight. No thanks. You never know who might be hanging around the machine.

Cash is fine and I've taken it, anyway." She smiled. "Helps with the motive, anyway."

Su-lin went back to her bag and pulled out a magazine in a sealed plastic cover. She opened it carefully with her gloved hands and approached the man on the bed. "Kinky stuff, eh Jerry?" The magazine was hard core bondage material, Japanese in origin. She went on: "Now Jerry, you're going to be a very good boy now or I might just cut a little deeper. I'm going to put the magazine first into you left hand and then into your right. All I want you to do is to grip it gently a few times. Think you can manage that? Oh and don't be silly and try to rip it or I really will take a tiny piece of you in return. All right?

He nodded, slowly and extended the fingers of both bound wrists as Su-lin allowed him to leave his fingerprints on the magazine in the places where they were likely to be left by the average reader "More props Jerry, I really should have been a stage manager, don't you think?" Jerry said nothing but he was having difficulty in controlling his breathing. He thought that now the woman was starting to talk, he might have more of a chance: he had read somewhere that hostage takers were less likely to kill their victims if they started to talk to them. His throat was dry with fear and his attempt at normal speech was scratchy and forced.

"Listen, I don't know what it is you want but you probably don't know how wealthy I am. Well, I'll tell you. According to my accountant, I'm worth rather more than 200 million dollars. You can have half of that.

"Only half, Jerry? Come on, you're not in a good bargaining position. What about three quarters?"

"Yes, all right;150 million, its yours." She was amused

"Just joking, Jerry. You see, it's not really possible, is it? How would we do it? Go to the bank together while you obediently transfer it to my account? Cash? Buy some diamonds together? Then you wave good-bye whilst I walk cheerfully onto the jet foil?" She shook her head. "Good try but we both know what would happen: your hired thugs would have me minus the money at the bottom of the harbour before I'd walked ten yards."

"Look, I promise you wouldn't be harmed. I'll even sign a statement promising the money was a gift to you and..."

No, Jerry." She scowled now. "Your promise? Signed statements? Desperate stuff and anyway I wouldn't trust you as far as I could spit. Anyway, its time to look at my family album and I think you've probably said enough." She stood up and walked towards the table. Taking a squash ball and a roll of adhesive tape from her bag, she returned to the bed.

"Now Jerry. Open your mouth. Its up to you, if you don't do as I say I'll put a hole in your windpipe. Either way, I don't want to hear another word." Cringing at the thought of the scalpel, Lai reluctantly opened his mouth.

"Good boy." She placed the ball inside the man's mouth and covered his lips with a strip of tape, then pulled a thick photograph album from her bag. "Now, I'm sure you're dying to know what the photographs are so let's get started."

She opened the book and started the commentary. The first page showed a young man and women holding hands. They were standing in front of an imposing building. "This is Tony Tse and me at Hong Kong University. We're both in our final year. He was studying law and I medicine. We had met two years before and become lovers very shortly after." More pictures followed. Tse and Su-lin at the Po Lin monastery, on a beach together, in front of a temple that could only have been in Bangkok and outside the funicular railway station in Penang, always smiling, always touching. More of the same followed. Occasionally other young couples appeared and once the two were with an older man and woman, presumably the parents of one of the two lovers. Some of the photographs showed only one of the pair but usually both were in shot.

"We had the most glorious two years together and no-one, not even you." She shot a glance of almost obscene malevolence at Lai, "Not even you can take that away." She regained her composure and turned the page. This time the couple were dressed in caps and gowns, holding parchment scrolls. There were several such pictures: individually, in groups and with each other.

"Graduation day. That was fun and then, in the evening, Tony proposed and I accepted." Another picture, the laughing couple embracing in a restaurant.

"We didn't want a long engagement and so the wedding was set for August. My father was a big noise in the Anglican community so we had it at the Cathedral, the reception at the Mandarin." Glittering photographs of the newlyweds and guests at both venues followed

"Then the honeymoon. Oh, neither family was in your league but both were wealthy enough and so we went overseas." She turned the page and photographs obviously taken in Canada and the States appeared. Su-lin's voice softened and a dreamy smile softened her features.

Then the hard glitter was back, her mouth compressed in thin line but the voice was still light, although there was a brittleness about it.

With sickening realisation, Lai now knew the woman was mad. She went on.

"Well, Jerry, I don't need to tell you that we had family in Canada and the USA. After all, what Hong Kong family doesn't?" The pages turned. Mount Whistler, Vancouver, the Seattle Tower, the Golden Gate. Disneyland, Universal Studios. Su-lin looked up and spoke apologetically:

"I do hope I'm not boring you, other peoples' photographs can be very dull but please be patient, we're nearly there." Lai pulled surreptitiously at the rope on his right wrist: the one she couldn't see but the bitch was sharp and spoke as if as if to a wayward child.

"Now then, Jerry, that's very naughty. I told you not to struggle. If you do it again I'll slice the tendon in your elbow which would be very messy and rather painful." He subsided, fear threatening to overwhelm him. She turned the page.

It was still in America and the location was unmistakable: Las Vegas. There was a bizarre similarity between the garish lights and false glamour of the gambling capital and the woman. Perhaps it was the superficial attraction or. more likely the corrupt purpose behind the glittering facade. The city existed to destroy those who went there, dazzled by its colourful promise. Su-lin, ravishing and semi-naked, smiled at Lai across the open album, the scalpel beside her with the blood now blackening and hardening on the shiny blade. Her tone became flat and hard.

"This is where things went wrong, you see. I had never known Tony gamble before but we went out to one of the casinos. Very smart and beautifully run. Much better than the tacky ones here in Macau. There we were, just newlyweds, having fun. A quick flutter and back to the hotel. Well, that was the idea but it didn't work out like that." Again, her thoughts shifted, covering years and continents. Slowly, she returned to the present.

"We had our first row that evening. Tony wanted to stay and gamble and I left in a huff. I thought he'd follow in a few minutes but it was three in the morning before he came back to the hotel room. He'd lost 10,000 American dollars. Well, he was bitterly ashamed, especially since that was about all the savings he had. He apologised time and again and promised he was through with gambling. Of course, I forgave him and why not? He was an intelligent, well balanced individual and I thought it was a one off, which it was. For a time." She flipped over another page.

Tse and Su-lin again. This time he was in police uniform, receiving an award from a much beribboned senior officer. "Tony decided that he wanted to practice at the criminal bar and he felt that most lawyers had far too little direct experience with what he called 'the hard end of the business'. In his opinion, most criminal lawyers had no background knowledge of those they prosecuted or defended so Tony decided to do a few years as a cop. He breezed through the training course and took the baton of honour as the best recruit inspector." She sighed: "I was so proud of him, that day."

"I started my internship and Tony did a year in uniform before asking for a transfer to CID, which nobody did. There was a bit of glamour about the detective stuff but the hours were very irregular and incredibly long. Still, it was what Tony wanted and he was doing well, at first." More photos, Tony receiving commendations and newspaper clippings of arrests and successful court cases. Su-lin glance at Lai and said conversationally: "I met a judge at a cocktail party at the university once. He told me Tony was the best prosecution witness he had ever seen. Always well prepared, totally honest, spoke fluently and never ever got rattled by the defence. Well, he certainly had me fooled."

"Because, sometime during his CID time, he'd started gambling again. I didn't notice at first because I was working hard at my internship and there being only the two of us, money wasn't a problem. Anyway, our lives were about to change again. What do you think of this picture?" Again, the handsome young couple but there was a roundedness to Su-lin and Tony, whilst smiling broadly, looked thin and haggard."

"Yes, I was pregnant but just then, at what should have been the happiest time of our lives, things started going wrong. Tony kept getting mysterious phone calls. Sometimes people would call during the night. If I answered, they'd hang up."

"Then Tony sold his car. He loved that car and had almost paid it off. When I asked why, he just shrugged his shoulders and said it wasn't big enough for the baby. Well, that was true, I suppose but when I asked what he was going to get instead he went shifty and said he'd think about it"

He seemed to be working all hours and was exhausted most of the time but a mutual friend, woman inspector, confided to me that she thought Tony was overdoing it and needed a rest because his work was getting sloppy. Of course, he denied it and I believed him until that day." She turned over the page and this time, there was a newspaper cutting.

"Mid Levels Rape and Burglary"

"Sometime last night, unknown men broke into flat in Robinson Road, ransacking the contents. Apparently, they were disturbed during the break-in by the wife of the owner, who was five months pregnant. The woman, who cannot be named, was injured during the attack which left the flat, according to neighbours, 'like a battlefield.' Rumours that the flat belonged to a senior detective have not been confirmed and a police spokesman asked that the matter be left to the authorities and no attempt made to trace the whereabouts of the woman. "This was an utterly repellent attack and we are absolutely determined to bring the offenders to justice," he said.

"Well, Jerry, those two were waiting for me; it was no accident. You wouldn't believe what they'd done, or maybe you would. Everything smashed, mattresses ripped and shit smeared all over the walls but they'd done all that before I arrived and they must have done it quietly too, since none of the neighbours heard any-thing. Anyway, I came back from my ante natal class at 10.30 and they let me get inside before they grabbed me."

"Tales of rape probably bore you, Jerry. You're probably one of the 'well she was asking for it. dressed like that' school but I was-n't 'dressed like that'. I was coming home from a class, dressed in a maternity smock. They didn't mind. They were quick and knew what they were doing. One of them grabbed me by the arms whilst the other hit me twice in the face and once in the stomach. I wasn't fully unconscious but I everything seemed unreal. Perhaps it was a defence mechanism. I don't know whether i lost the baby then or during the rape but by the time they left, the contractions were starting. Before they went, one of them said to me: 'Tell your husband this counts as the first instal-ment. If he wants to discuss less painful ways to pay, tell him to go to the 'Painted Lady' in Lockhart Road at eight to-morrow night and ask for Shum Jai. If he's not there, we'll come back for you' I managed to call for the ambulance and ring Tony's mobile. I don't remember very much except that the miscarriage hap-pened before anyone arrived. So much blood and that, that pathetic little thing, not moving. I passed out then." She sighed. Lai was rapt."

"Tony got to the hospital almost the same time as me. Other police were there but Tony knew the man in charge and they let him speak to me, in spite of the doctors being reluctant. Anyway, I insisted. I told him what they had said and somehow, although he was shocked and horrified by what had happened, he didn't seem surprised. He squeezed my hand, told me he loved me and made me promise not to tell anyone else what the man had said. Then they gave me an injection and I slept. The next day was a blur. Jerry stayed for an hour but said little. My parents looked in and were horrified and a woman officer came to take a statement. She was very nice but I told her I couldn't remember very much of the attack and in truth I couldn't. It came back slowly over the next few days and now of course, its crystal clear.

"Am I boring you? Never mind, not long now. The next page contained two short newspaper cuttings. One told of a murder in the New Territories where the body of a man suffering from sev-eral gunshot wounds, had been found floating in a reservoir whilst the other reported a dead man in a Wanchai back street, his throat slashed. In both cases, anonymous police sources had inferred the dead men had triad backgrounds.

The penultimate document was a typed letter.

My Darling Su-lin

I am writing this because I doubt I would have had the courage to tell you. Briefly, I knew who was responsible for this before you gave me the message. As you probably guessed, it was gambling. Once I had got the taste for it in Vegas, I couldn't seem to give it up. I stopped at the training school but once I was out, especially in CID it was just too tempting.

One of the boys introduced me to this casino in Macau and it seemed not too bad a place, as these places went and it started to become regular haunt. At first, I won, enough to pay off the car in fact but then it started to go wrong. I know it was stupid but the only thing I'll say in my defence is that the betting was rigged. Small consolation but credit was easy, or so I thought. Then, one night, when you thought I was on duty, a couple of the security guards invited me to go to the boss's office. It was all very polite and the boss was all smiles. Did I know how much I owed the casino? I was staggered at the amount, more than a million Hong Kong. The man's name was Lai. Jerry Lai, big smiling smarmy bastard. He felt I might have difficulty repaying and he could help

All he needed was the odd piece of information about police actions. You see, he had friends in Hong Kong who were running a few harmless betting operations and the like and advance warnings of police raids would help matters considerably. Since I was working in Wanchai, surely such information would be easy to come by. I told him where to go and his smile never faltered. How then, did I propose to settle the debt, which was after all, rising at ten per cent daily? He showed me the credit agreement i had signed. I was hooked and the bastard knew it.

I came back and started working for Jerry Lai. I used all my contacts and often managed to pass on details of a planned raid. I never knew who I was telling, it was just a mobile phone number. Then one day, I got a call. As you probably guessed, it was Shum Jai. I already knew of him as a local triad member and a rent boy. He told me Jerry had an important message for me. It was quite simple, Jerry wanted more information. I was to engineer myself a transfer to the vice squad where I would be in a far better position to obtain and pass on information. He knew and

Christ knows how, that vacancies existed in the squad and I should apply without delay.

Well, that's when things went really wrong. Finally, I could see the inevitability. I would get my transfer and start tipping Lai's boys off in earnest. It wouldn't take long before my failure rate became blindingly obvious. Suspicion would lead to an internal investigation and then a criminal prosecution. Quite simply. I'd had it. I told Shum Jai to stuff it. He grinned nastily and said he felt Mr. Lai wouldn't be pleased and anyway they had enough on me to get me arrested anyway. I walked out.

Please believe me when I say I never thought they'd move so fast and go for you like that. I was expecting another call with a slightly different offer - that's the way the sods usually operate.

Anyway, as soon as I left the hospital the second day, I went to the meeting. Shum was there, along with his mate. I sat down and asked what they wanted me to do. Shum told me that was better and was about to tell me something when I interrupted:

"Shum Jai, I've got my revolver pointed at your balls. You do exactly as I say or I'll blow them off and believe me, I'd really enjoy it." Darling, just seeing the blood drain from his nasty mean little face made me feel better than I'd felt for days. I knew I'd got to him when a pool of urine started spreading around his feet. "Now, just you tell your friend to meet us outside in five minutes. Look confident and in control or I'll pull the trigger. Don't worry, I'm not going to kill you." I think he believed. He wanted to, of course. How he managed it I don't know but he passed the message tersely enough. Then we walked out, him in front. On my instructions we turned into an alleyway.

When you look in your medical kit, you'll find your big dissecting knife missing. Don't worry, nobody will ever find it. It was very simple. I told him to turn around and as he did so, I pulled the knife out from my right sleeve, where it had been held by elastic bands and slashed his throat. I'd never killed before but there was no compunction. He was a sleazy rapist with as criminal record a yard long. Strangely he didn't seem hurt, just surprised and that was the expression he had on his face when he died.

The alleyway was dark when the other man came out. It wasn't difficult to give a fair imitation of Shum's voice and when I said: "Now, you dumb cop, you'll do as you're told" the other man fell for it. I heard him get close, then spun and smashed him across the jaw with my revolver. Before he could recover I told him Shum was dead and that if he wanted to live, he and I were going for a drive in his car. I knew he had one of course: all those triads like a flash car to impress the girls.

I think he knew he was going to die but he had guts, more than his friend but I wanted to get things straight. We drove to a reservoir, miles from anywhere, then we talked. At first he didn't want to but then I shot him in the knee. He started talking then. It had been Lai's orders, he said. He and Shum were to threaten me once more and then they would kill you if I didn't co-operate. They weren't going to rush, they'd probably wait until you were out of hospital. They knew I couldn't protect you all the time. He said that Lai had gained enormous face from his tip offs and the clients were paying handsomely. He needed me at least until he could get another sucker.

The last thing he said was that he had enjoyed raping you and that he would do it again anytime. That's when I shot him in the balls. The last shot went into his face. I shoved him in the reservoir and drove back to town. Back to our flat. I hadn't really tried to clean it up.

Darling. I can never be sorry enough for what I've done to you and to us. The only thing I don't regret is killing those two scum who raped you. The world is better without them

Please try to forgive me

All my love

Tony.

"I got this letter in hospital. Shortly afterwards the nice woman inspector called and broke the news to me that Tony was dead, believed to have committed suicide in his office. Apparently there were two shots left. Each one had hit." She seemed to find this funny.

The last item in the album was a brief newspaper report of Tony's suicide.

"And that's really about it, Jerry. It wasn't difficult to find you but I waited a decent interval, needed to get my life back on track, think things over. You see, Jerry, you're really even worse than the two who raped me and killed my baby: they're just mindless thugs but you and others like you, you prey on weakness and even then you're not satisfied. You squeeze the life out of people and destroy the lives of everyone around them."

"Anyway, that's enough time wasted. You must be really keen

to know what happens next. Well its very simple." She went back to the table and took out a syringe. "This is filled with digitalis and will give you a massive heart attack. I doubt anybody will investigate too closely. After all, its obvious what happened. You, an overweight middle aged man who smoke and drank too much, indulged in kinky sex with a casino prostitute. Too bad but the casino will be keen to cover up the case - bad for business - and your partners will be keen to get back to work. So Jerry, this is the last present you're going to get and its more than you deserve - a quick death but at least you'll die knowing." She approached, intending to inject the contents into his penis beneath the foreskin, where a cursory examination would miss it.

Lai was now beyond terror. His body convulsed, his eyes bulged and then softened into death. Fear had preempted chemical. Su-lin quickly replaced the syringe, and changed into spare clothes, pinning up her hair and donning thick spectacles. In two minutes the ravishing prostitute had disappeared and a dowdy cleaner packed her bag and left the hotel.

Su-lin had been right: there had been little fuss in the papers and the death had been to due to heart failure. As most deaths ultimately were, she mused, reading the two line report in her office. She buzzed her secretary. "Is my next patient her, Stella?"

"Yes Doctor."

"Send her in. please."

The woman who came in was haggard, her face bruised. Su-lin's counselling clinic for victims of rape and violence was well known and her own experiences gave her an empathy with her patients fortunately denied to most doctors. Her patients confided in her and she was often able to help. Some of the women had been assaulted by persons known who had subsequently been arrested. Other were victims of domestic violence and the victims reluctant to report the matter to the police. By careful questioning, she was able to discover the haunts and habits of some of these violent and ruthless men. Three of them had subsequently met a glamourous woman in her thirties. None had survived the encounter and the police had in no instance found suspicious circumstances.

Of course, as Su-lin frequently told herself, there are things other than healing that doctors can do so well. She coughed. Soon, she would have to go into hospital herself.

She had had two other successes, both men who had been known to their victims but had terrified them sufficiently to ensure their silence. These, Su-lin had dealt with differently. Both had been successfully seduced but not until a detailed and anonymous dossier of evidence had been dispatched to the police, together with an anonymous phone call which had resulted in the offender's arrest just after his last night of passion. Su-lin had let these live. She had no need to kill them. Shum Jai's legacy would kill them as surely as it was killing her and she was always careful to ensure that the authorities were tipped off that their latest arrest was an AIDS carrier.

Some of Su-lin's colleagues had often wondered why she never gave blood and all of them were concerned about her failing health. But she was tired she would say, just tired and soon she would rest.

Ghost Writer

by
M M Lee

M M Lee

M M Lee has worked for the United Nations (in Geneva and Vienna) in the field of human rights, disaster relief, protection of children, and social development. She spent a year as a public information consultant for the shipping industry in Papua New Guinea.

At present she is plotting her third novel and has completed a novel and series of short stories for children.

One of her short stories was shortlisted for the Ian St James Award 1996 and was published in the December 1996/January 1997 issue of THE NEW WRITER.

She lives in France.

Ghost Writer

by

M M Lee

The wretched woman stayed stubbornly unaware of me, whatever I did. I made stairs creak, doors slam, windows rattle; I howled in the chimney.

"I hadn't realised it was so windy today," she'd murmur to herself, smoothing her always immaculate fair hair.

I knocked vases off tables, ornaments off ledges; I broke wine glasses.

"Must be getting clumsy in my old age." She'd say with a shrug.

Old age? Forty's nothing; wait until you've been around as long as I have I'd whisper like a far-off echo in a dream. This was much too subtle.

So I moved things around: books from table to floor, pens from desk to windowsill; I hung towels in the dining-room.

"Must have been daydreaming." She'd smile to herself.

You see the problem? She had no imagination, none at all. From the moment she arrived I was aware of that. Which is why I used only my most basic arts. Naturally, I reserve my finer effects for the more worthy, those with a developed sense of the spooky. For it is, I find, quite impossible to raise enthusiasm for frightening anyone who lacks a delight in being scared. Where's the fun? There is none. And there should be. No, she had to be got out of the house - she was only a tenant after all - so that someone of a more fanciful disposition could move in. Fair's fair.

If I couldn't scare her away by simple means, I had, reluctantly, to become more obvious; my reputation depended on it. And that's another thing. It is extremely irritating the way houses commandeer such reputations: words like 'haunted' or 'atmospheric' are applied to *them* without, I insist, any justification whatsoever. They just sit there, houses, they don't actually *do* anything. It is both annoying and unfair that some of them are spoken of with fear and awe, when it's me and my kind who should receive such splendid accolades.

Anyway, back to this woman who was not, I hasten to assure you, hard of hearing or short-sighted; she was just depressingly unimaginative. You could tell that by the amount of television she watched. She'd sit there, night after night, staring at the screen, legs curled up on her favourite chair, at hand a glass of Chablis to sip languidly, a dish of almonds to eat daintily. And a silly smile on her face if it was that fatuous series starring Tom Vane. I think he appealed to her; what she expected to do about it I haven't the least glimmer, or interest. But I shouldn't be hard on poor old Tom Vane, for his series gave me the idea of going where she couldn't fail to notice me - into the television set! Pity it's not possible, in my world, to patent or protect ideas: no unions, that's the trouble.

So, having flung a few cushions about the place, banged a window here and there, and generally tried to create the right atmosphere, I popped into the set just before she switched on to prevent her thinking the set was faulty straight away. And I waited patiently until Tom was about to take his latest leading lady into his hairy arms.

With a shudder of anticipation, I used my ability to take on any form I desire, and outlined myself around Tom in a white on black image, like a negative. The more frequent phenomenon is, of course, a colourless outline; but I decided my choice would be more effective. I heard her sigh with irritation as she fiddled with the buttons on the remote control. She gave up, frantic at missing the programme. Deepening my negative image I stood out even more, especially around his face; she will keep insisting he has a tantalising mouth. This time she tried the knobs on the set itself. Nothing worked.

Then, just as Tom had his latest playmate in a firm grip, I

made him scratch his nose. I mean, of course, that *his* nose stayed unwrinkled, and I scratched *mine*. She didn't notice at first - perhaps she does need glasses. As he continued his amorous onslaught, I lifted my face and shook my head slowly, in a most disinterested manner. I'd caught her attention. She leant forward. I yawned. She uncurled her legs. I coughed, silently of course. She picked up her glass; her hand had just the slightest tremor.

Meanwhile, Tom was still in his clinch, the woman swooning away, both of them probably wondering what they'd be having for dinner. Excuse the cynicism, but I can't believe such scenes are supposed to be taken seriously. They are *meant* to be funny - aren't they?

By now she was ... puzzled, let's put it no higher than that. Before her very eyes she could see Tom Vane in a passionate embrace, and me, his alter ego, bored with the whole affair.

I think I finally began to get through to her when I combed my hair, which I did with as much arm and neck-stretching panache as possible. Me upright, Tom nearly prone by his time. She was decidedly bothered, revealed by the way she changed channels abruptly, then switched back and peered at the screen, sideways on. I was still there - picking my teeth ostentatiously. She grabbed the television guide and flicked through it at a furious pace. If she'd hoped for comfort there she didn't find any.

Sometimes the silliest things can be the most effective. With Tom and his partner now completely prone, I arose, hitched up one shoulder, backed away and then, in a rush, leapfrogged over them both.

For a while she sat motionless gazing at the wall, then she stood up, very slowly, and walked to the cabinet to stare hard at the bottle of Chablis. It was nearly full.

Then, just as Tom and his lady were moving into the bedroom, and I had broken into a spectacular dance routine, she switched off the set and picked up the telephone. She rang the television studio.

"Tell me," she said with commendable calm, "has there been an undisclosed decision to experiment on the Tom Vane programme this evening?"

She received a rude, or at least negative, response from someone, judging by the flush that flooded her face.

With her hair now decidedly rumpled, she tried a friend. "Was he by any chance watching Tom Vane? ... No? Would he mind switching over and having a look, there was something odd going on. Thank you so much! ... Nothing wrong with your picture? But, truly, there was something very strange happening on mine .... There's no need to be rude! Tom Vane's a very attractive man - there are few of them around!"

I'll draw a shroud over the rest; it was embarrassing rather than amusing to listen to her being angry at someone else. I was seeking her undivided attention.

She went straight to bed (see what I mean about lack of imagination!) but didn't sleep at all well. She rang the local television shop first thing, before breakfast.

"What seems to be the problem?" Asked the repair man when he arrived an hour or so later. I allowed her to deal with him and faded into the curtains behind the television.

"A double image on the screen, though I don't suppose that's the correct technical term." She said apologetically.

"Not to worry, missus. Let's have a look." She excused herself and went to make coffee. I stayed; what goes on inside a television set is utterly *fantastic* - my highest compliment. He gave the set a complete overhaul; how pleasant it is to watch another professional at work. Sadly, I seldom if ever have the satisfaction of seeing *my* efforts applauded. But one can't have everything, in this world or the next, regrettably. It will not, I feel sure, surprise you to learn that he could find no fault at all with the set.

Perhaps he took pity on her agitated disbelief, or perhaps he was simply a well-meaning man, for he took the time to tell her the technical reason for the images she'd complained of: a reflection of the transmitting waves in optical systems. This meant nothing at all to her. Still, she smiled with a brave attempt at intelligence. Then she did react as he added, in an aside:

"Mind you, the usual cause of that kind of interference is a defect in the receiver. In the trade, we call them ghosts."

How right he was - on both counts. Though he hardly noticed how she started at this remark.

She pondered long and hard after his departure. The upshot? Well, that evening she had obviously decided not to switch on the television. She made herself conspicuously busy. But let me be fair: around ten o'clock she showed a certain amount of courage by leaping up and switching on. Need I tell you? I was there, entwined around the head and shoulders of the most serious television news presenter, waving at her. She announced, *very* loudly, that she needed a holiday.

Now, even though it was on that very holiday that she met the man of her dreams and married him, I insist that I was the catalyst in getting her out of the house.

My success was qualified, however, by the penalty points that now sully my hitherto untarnished record. Why was I punished rather than praised you ask? Because of the finicky structure of our rating system. I was chastised because the wretched woman failed to give me any credit for her departure from the house. (I have it on good authority that she never even mentioned me to her husband; hardly an auspicious beginning to a truthful relationship, surely?) Far more deplorable - so our judging panel decided - was that my triumph involved the use of a medium not only of the artificial variety, but one that had stolen an elemental term of our profession.

But I remain undaunted, and I must say I have high hopes of the incoming tenant. This one looks much more promising - he already bites his nails.

©M M Lee

The Mystery of Jack the Ripper Resolved

by
Ian Williams

Ian Williams

Ian was born in 1958, in the Borough of Bromley, which is the same borough where H G Wells was born: a fact that both inspires and weighs heavily on him. He still lives in Bromley, and works by day as a VAT Assurance Officer (a fancy name for a VAT Inspector), and at night, amongst other pastimes such as cinema going and listening to music, he writes short stories.

He has appeared in various publications including The First Saffron Short Story Collection and The Platform.

The Mystery of Jack the Ripper Resolved

by

Ian Williams

On a chill December evening in 1888, Liz Brodie pulled a threadbare shawl around her shoulders, and wondered why the streets of Whitechapel had become deserted. Maybe it was because of the bitter cold; or perhaps it was the dense fog drifting over the East End of London? Whatever the reason, business was bad and Liz was contemplating having to go home penniless, when a cough from behind startled her. Liz spun round, and saw a man step out of a narrow passageway. She wondered how long he had been there.

"Looking for company?" she asked.

"What're you charging?" He replied.

"Depends what you want."

"The usual."

"It's one bob, then."

"Okay. Is your place far from here?"

"A couple of streets on."

She took his arm and lead the way as if they were a couple. Only the stiffness of the man and their differing ages gave any hint of illicitness. The fog had thickened and the houses on the other side of the street had disappeared. In the dull silence of the fog, their footsteps echoed.

"Thick, innit?" said Liz.

"Walking through this fog is like walking through pure evil. This is where our worst nightmares dwell and find form."

"Yes." She said, unconcerned by his strangeness. After all her years on the game, she was no longer surprised by either how ordinary or how strange her clients were. *Think of 'em purely as walkin' wallets*, Nick had once said. And so she did.

As they passed a street lamp, she took a quick glance at him. He wore a thick over-coat, which made him look bigger than he actually was, and bowler hat. He was tall and lean, with a weak chin and a long nose. His eyes were furtive; but then that could be said for most of her clients.

They walked on in silence until they arrived at a house. "This way." She said, and lead him into a passage, up some stairs and across a landing. She opened a door to a flat - it wasn't locked - and they both walked in. She closed the door behind them. This time she locked it.

She lit a paraffin lamp that sat on a chest of drawers. The weak light illuminated the dingy surroundings. An iron bedstead with a pot beneath it; a wash basin standing in a corner; and a bare fire-place with an empty mantelpiece. A second door lead into another room. The walls, like so many poor dwellings, had neither paper nor paint on them and although the light was too dim to show the dampness, the smell was unmistakable.

"Pay me the shilling now and then you can undress."

The transaction carried out, he took off his bowler and placed it on the bed.

"I'll be back in a minute." She said, turning to leave.

He faced the bed and started unbuttoning his coat. A creaking floorboard made him turn around. A brawny thug over six feet tall stepped menacingly towards him, wielding an iron bar. The client instinctively stepped back: his once furtive eyes now wide in terror. He threw up his arms to protect himself as the iron bar swung down. There was a soggy crunching sound as it smashed into his skull. He slumped to the floor.

The thug loomed over his victim, the blood stained bar gripped tightly in his hand ready to strike again. Liz peered cautiously at the body. She could tell by the eyes- wide open and lifeless- that he was dead.

"Its all right, Nick," she said. "He's a goner. Let's see what he's got."

Nick produced a rag from his coat pocket and wiped the blood off the iron bar. He knelt down, placing the bar on the floor, and went through his victim's pockets.

"Nothing in 'is pockets apart from the usual knick-knacks," he said. "But there's something under his coat. Let's take it off and have a look."

He unbuttoned the coat and pulled it open. Arranged neatly on the inside of the coat were six leather pouches sewn on to the lining. In each pouch there was a knife. Liz and Nick stared at the knives transfixed.

"Oh God!" She said. "It's him. The Ripper!"

Nick rose up and stepped away from the body, not a little in awe. "Jack the Ripper," he said, incredulously. "No, I don't believe it."

"What do you think those knives are for, idiot!" She screamed, fighting a losing battle to control her rising hysteria. She turned her face towards the wall and burst into tears. She had been *that* close to being the seventh victim of Jack the Ripper.

"We could make a fortune out of this," Nick said, his mind turning on this bit of good luck. "Do you know the police have got a £500 reward out on him?"

She turned to glare at him. "Are you stupid? How are we to explain him being in my flat with his head smashed in?"

"We could concoct a story."

"And what if the police don't believe our story? What if they start asking questions about the other silly sods we've done in? If we turn up with the body of Jack the Ripper, and he's got exactly the same wounds on his head as the others, they're bound to start putting two and two together."

"Not necessarily."

"Is it worth the risk?"

Nick looked at the body, turning over in his mind what Liz had said. "You're right," he said reluctantly. "You're absolutely right. I'll strip him of his valuables then I'll dump him in the Thames . . .just like the others."

Nick went into the next room and reappeared with a packing crate and an oilcloth. He spread the oilcloth out in the middle of

77

the floor. He lifted up the body, and together with Liz, who had recovered her composure, stripped it of all its clothes. Soon it was naked. Liz went into the next room to rummage through the clothes looking for valuables. Nick stayed in the room to saw the body up so that it would fit into the packing crate. When she came out, he was mopping up blood from the oilcloth. The body was already in the box. She could never stay in the room while Nick dismembered a corpse.

"Did we get much?" He asked.

"Twenty pound in cash, a gold watch and a leather wallet."

"And some knives."

"Yeah, knives too."

"Not bad at all. Nice clothes. Should get a good price for them alone. And as for those knives- did you see them? - they must be worth a small fortune."

"Nick, throw the knives away. It's too risky taking them to a pawnbroker."

"Liz, no. Those knives are worth a fortune . . . and we need the money."

"What if the pawnbroker gets suspicious if the knives turn up just as the Ripper-murders stop? It might bring the police to our front door. The last thing we want to do is draw attention to ourselves."

"Okay," he said. "Still, it's a shame. They look like an expensive set."

A week later, Liz passed a pawnbroker while on her way to visit her mother in Hackney. A gleam caught her eye in the pawnbroker's window. She stopped in her tracks and stared in horror. *The bloody fool*, she thought, panic threatening to overwhelm her, that greedy stupid bloody fool!

Before her, laid out for display in the window were the tools of Jack the Ripper. Six gleaming knives, each a different size but all of a set, going for a snip at two guineas.

©Ian Williams

Forgive Me

by
Gary Orchard

Gary Orchard

Gary lives in Southampton with his wife Jackie and two cats, Ziggy and Baldrick. Following a varied career as a sound engineer, DJ, musician and lyricist he became an actor and playwright with the Komikazee Theatre Company. For the past ten years he has been their Artistic Director and Writer in Residence producing many one-act and full length plays in the Hampshire Area. His first novel, a macabre thriller called 'CHARLATAN' was published in 1995. He is currently working on the screenplay adaptation of his award winning stage production of 'AN EVENING WITH ROSIE'.

Forgive Me

by
Gary Orchard

I love my wife.

It's really as simple as that. But for the longest time I told myself I did not. Once we'd parted, I did my utmost to pretend she did not exist. But somewhere deep inside I knew that with each passing day I was missing her more, loving her more and yet I still denied it. Only now, when she haunts my thoughts every waking moment, when her memory warms me through the cold, empty nights, have I finally come to my senses.

I still remember her words on our wedding night.

"I was born to be yours," she said, her head a gentle weight against my shoulder, her breath warm against my skin. "I have never loved, nor will ever love anyone as much as you."

I smiled, as I recall, embarrassed and pleased that I could incite such devotion. I pray now that she meant it and has not found comfort with someone else during my absence, but at the time I simply accepted it like the vain fool I certainly was.

Not that I was unhappy at the start. Far from it. Those first few months with Elizabeth were as close to idyllic as mortal man can hope for. But, as time passed, I began to get restless. I wanted more, you see. I wanted to experience all that life had to offer and I became more and more frustrated with the petty restrictions of my existence.

Elizabeth was patient with me, supportive and encouraging, but deep in my heart I knew I was not destined for great things and that very thought began to fester and grow like a cancer.

And then I met Tara.

We met at a party. Elizabeth was ill and could not attend. She had urged me to go on my own so as not to miss out on the fun. It was her usual caring thoughtfulness, but, oh, Elizabeth, how bitterly I now regret leaving you alone that night.

When Tara entered the room I felt time stand still. All I could hear was the beating of my heart; all I could feel was the pounding of the blood in my veins; all I could see was her face, so sensual, so cruel, so irresistible.

Of course, I was not alone in my fascination. Every man in the room was jockeying for position to speak with her, to be blessed with a smile, a touch on the arm. Each and every one of them ready to abandon everything should she ask them to. But she didn't ask them.

She asked me.

I can still remember how amazed I was when she made her way over to me. I thought I would die. Perhaps it would have been better if I had done. But I didn't. Instead I stared, mesmerised. She smiled, amused, certain of her power to entrance. She leaned closer, flicking her tongue across even, white, teeth and scarlet lips and whispered in my ear.

"I want you."

That was all she said, all she needed to say, and I knew I was irretrievably hooked.

Within a week I had left Elizabeth and moved in with Tara. With Tara I felt born again. She taught me to see with newborn eyes, to experience the wonder of the world anew with senses sharpened to a pitch that was almost painful in its clarity. She lifted my spirit and introduced me to a world of sight, sound, touch and taste I had never dreamed existed. Her knowledge was encyclopedic, her energy boundless, her enthusiasm unquenchable and her will indomitable. Not that I ever tried to break away, not then.

Oh, no. I was a most willing pupil and Tara a most meticulous teacher. She absorbed me completely into her world and introduced me to her friends. They accepted me, some grudgingly, others with genuine affection, as though I were a pet or some new toy of which she would soon tire. It frightened but did not surprise me to learn that I was not her first protegé.

"You are very special," she told me. "I knew as soon as I saw you. You're not like the others. We were meant to be together and I'll never leave you."

If the words had a familiar ring to them I refused to acknowledge it. My wedding night, when Elizabeth had said almost those same words, was now a fleeting shadow of a dream that came infrequently in the depths of sleep.

To my undying shame I set about forgetting that Elizabeth had ever existed. I had no time to dwell on the past when Tara waited to guide me through the uncharted terrain of an exciting future. For the first time in my life I was living to the full. I saw things from a new perspective. Everything was wonderful and bright. I learned to appreciate the finest and the simplest of things under Tara's careful tutelage. Nothing was too grand or too complicated, nothing was mundane or ordinary, everything was to be enjoyed.

I embraced this hedonistic, selfish lifestyle with a will. I devoured art, literature, music, everything that came my way like a starving man presented with a feast. And by far the most exotic of all the delights that Tara lay before me were the pleasures of the flesh.

Never before had I known that such passion was possible. Tara pampered and instructed me, taking me to ever higher plains of desire, always leaving me craving more. A hopeless addict, I grew dependent on her caress, pined for her touch, craved only to please her in any way that I could in hopes of winning her approval, of achieving some reward.

I was a poor, blind fool, I can see that now, but at the time I didn't even stop to think. Whatever the excess, I was willing to partake if she did but say the word. I saw only through the eyes of a bewitched child, spellbound by a wonderful new toy.

I didn't notice the change until it was too late. When the caresses became harsher, the excesses tainted and obscure, the passion twisted and blighted. I never questioned, never faltered in my devotion. Not even when she urged me to initiate others into our most sacred and perverted practices. Somehow it seemed only natural. Such delights, such endless pleasure should be shared, not hoarded like a miser's gold.

It took a long time to see the tarnish on that particular crock of gold, but see it I did. Not with the startling revelation that had struck me when Tara and I first met. Oh, no, this was more insidious, a creeping realisation that such an existence, based solely on physical pleasure, is hollow and empty, a mockery of a true relationship. When even Tara could not teach me any more permutations on our endless theme of enjoyment I began to see the truth. And I began to think of Elizabeth.

A sane man would have told me I was on a fool's errand. Maybe so, but it was madness that drove us apart and I prayed to the God who must surely have abandoned me countless years ago that my current madness would bring us back together again.

I truly was a madman as I searched the half remembered streets of my youth, tracking her down, following the clues that finally led me here, to my beloved Elizabeth.

I stand before her now, a penitent sinner with no hope of redemption. For fifty years she has lain here beneath this cold, grey slab. Time moves so differently you see, for the creature I have become. For the creature Tara made of me and I had not realised. What price immortality if it cost you your soul and the woman you truly love?

I kneel now at Elizabeth's feet and pray for forgiveness as I wait for the dawn. As the first grey sliver of light appears I cry my first tears in nearly a century. Tears stained the rich, deep colour of blood.

©Gary Orchard

A Right Not To Know

by
Phil Cook

Phil Cook

Retirement from the Civil Service five years ago gave Phil Cook the time to develop his life-long interest in creative writing.

When he moved with his wife, Val, from Hampshire to North Yorkshire and joined the Ripon Writers' Group his efforts began to bear fruit. Fellow members encouraged him to submit his short stories to local radio: over sixty have been broadcast, many recorded by Phil himself. A selection, based on a travel theme, has recently been published in booklet form. Phil has also had a few short stories accepted by magazines and has achieved successes in various short story and poetry competitions.

A Right Not To Know

by

Phil Cook

"So you weren't just a dream. I was so afraid ..."

I had no proof - no photograph, no letter, no memento -that she had ever existed outside my dreams, the recurring dream that used to haunt me nightly.

In later years, friends looked sceptical when I asked, "Do you remember a girl called Helena I used to know?" But, of course, I had never mentioned her at the time. A shy, secretive youth, I would not have risked their mockery.

Had Helena told anyone about me? Probably not. And I doubt whether anyone ever saw us together. We melted into the landscape at the first sign of an intruder.

As the years passed, my memories, with nothing to support them, had merged with my dreams. Then even the dreams stopped.

Helena smiled at my half question, half statement. Her grey-green eyes radiated their special warmth. She understood my struggle for words in a tumult of remembered joy ... and pain.

"No, not a dream," she murmured, her voice as warm as the summer breeze.

I sighed. In that far-off summer, I thought everything would go on for ever: our new friendship, our shared discoveries about each other, about ourselves. How naïve to believe that anything lasted.

It was one of those summers when the sun shone all the time. Summers were like that when you were young.

"I knew you would come back ... one day," she said simply.

Could she have known that, after so many years, that dream of her had returned so vividly that I had had to make this pilgrimage? The dream had come out of the blue, but strangely comforting at a time when my ordered world was falling apart.

"You haven't changed," I said, marvelling. It sounded a cliché but was magnificently true. Well, almost. Faint lines around her eyes and across her forehead suggested a legacy of pain and stress.

I was glad she did not return "Nor have you." The shaving mirror tells the truth each morning.

"We all change," she responded, smiling gently. "But who's to say what we change from ... and to? Are we ever what we seem?"

I could not find the words I wanted, to tell her that her constancy was unique. In our all-too-short time together there had been no ambiguity in her feelings, no inexplicable swings of mood. The universal fickleness I had encountered in later life - and in which I had shared - had brought disappointment, despair. How different my life would have been with her.

"You were - are - the most wonderful person I ever met," I said, a banal expression of my deepest feelings.

But words were superfluous. Now, as before, I knew that Helena sensed my thoughts, my emotions.

We were walking by the stream in the woods as so often in that long summer holiday. We did not touch; I could not be so presumptuous, much as I longed to crush her in my arms. We pointed out remembered landmarks - the rustic bridge, the ruined forester's cottage, the gnarled oak under which ...

A sudden thought. How could she look so impossibly young? I glanced surreptitiously at her slim figure beneath a thin summer dress, her firm round breasts; at her light brown hair, simply worn, framing her lovely oval face, so pale but needing no artifice to enhance its natural beauty. Perhaps this was not Helena at all, but her daughter. Even ... my daughter?

Absurd. Only Helena could have known those intimate details.

We made love only that once. It was like a sacred seal on our friendship. Perhaps by then even I knew in my heart that the idyll, like the summer, must soon end.

I had been almost afraid to touch Helena during those six weeks, fearful I would somehow repel her. Occasionally we held hands briefly, or I kissed her cheek shyly. In a strange way I wanted her to remain untouched, even by me, so as not to put at risk the dream we shared. Yes, even then it seemed a dream. It was enough to be together, to share our love of the countryside, our inmost thoughts and fears and aspirations. Though it was mainly my plans that we spoke of, and she was content to give encouragement, help me crystallise my ideas.

Why rush things, why anticipate future joys, when the present was already so bountiful? I would have found it inconceivable then that we should not share the future.

But Helena, much wiser than I, perhaps realised that everything would quickly change; that it would be a cause for eternal regret if we did not seal our love. It was the hottest day of all, when she drew me to her as we lay under that oak tree. I still remember the elation ... and the guilt. Our lingering goodbye kiss - the first time I had kissed her lips - prolonged the magic.

I received her most precious gift on the last day of August, my eighteenth birthday. (And today, I suddenly remembered, was also my birthday. Was that pure chance?)

When she did not appear the following day, my exultation turned to grief. I never saw her again and presumed that my fears had been right. Had I so disappointed her that she could no longer bear to be with me?

Reading my thoughts as we gazed at silver fish darting between the reeds, Helena whispered, "I could not have borne to see you unhappy."

Her words made me ashamed of the harsh thoughts that had superseded my initial grief when she disappeared from my life. Surely she could have warned me, given some explanation, after everything we had shared?

By the time my fevered mind had become more rational it was too late. I knew none of the mundane details of her life - where she lived, what family she had or other friends, even her surname.

University and the wider world had swept me up, the opportunity of tracing Helena had gone. Other fish were fried ... and found wanting. My family moved house and I had finally settled down two hundred miles from my childhood haunts. There was no compelling reason to return; indeed, far better for my peace of mind to stay away.

"But why?" I asked, almost angrily, dropping twigs into the water as we stood on the stone pack horse bridge.

Her matter-of-fact eyes assessed my strength, even now, to accept the truth.

"The illness - the leukemia - had been in remission, but I could feel it was beginning again."

We were on the path by the stream again, approaching the village. I saw the church's Norman tower.

"Leukemia? But you never said anything about ..."

"What would be the point?"

"I could have come to you, helped to nurse you, cheered you up."

"You had already given me so much happiness, so many memories. They helped, they really did."

By now we were sitting on a bench in the walled graveyard, too public a place for us to have visited ... before.

"I had a right to know!" I almost shouted.

"You had a right not to know," she asserted firmly but gently. "How could I have spoiled your plans, all the things you were going to do; university, your career?"

"But only with you, for you. None of it mattered without you?" I cried. Then, when the turmoil had calmed, "Why didn't you try to get in touch ... when you recovered?"

That was what hurt most now I knew about her illness.

"Perhaps I did," she murmured. "You are here."

The silence that followed my outburst and her enigmatic reply was broken only by the gentle lowing of distant cattle and bees humming about their business. The scent of wild flowers and herbs was redolent of that far-off summer. Sadness welled up inside me at the wasted years. But now that I had found her I would never let Helena go again. There was still time to make up for all we had lost.

As she sat beside me, her lovely face betraying no emotion, I wondered whether she shared my thoughts, my sense of loss, my determination not to be parted again.

"Do you remember that wild rose you gave me ... that last day?" She asked at length, a dreamy smile on her face. As though I could forget! "Look at the roses over there."

I stood up and walked across to where she pointed. They were exactly the same as the one I had given her - pure white with the faintest tinge of pink, like her skin. And in joyous profusion.

"Come and look," I called, but she did not move.

A white stone stood behind the flowers and, ignoring the sharp thorns, I pushed the briars aside to read the inscription:

"HELENA MARLOWE, aged 17, who lost her brave battle against illness on 14 September 1966."

When I turned round, the bench was empty.

The Soul in the Wall

by
Sean Jeffery

Sean Jeffery

Some of Sean's other short stories have appeared in anthologies, and recently on the Internet. He also plays football, composes music and programs computers, with varying degrees of success. He is thirty years old and lives in Worcester with two cats and a wife.

The Soul in the Wall

by

Sean Jeffery

"Perhaps it's a riddle," said Alex as he studied the receipt.

"CENTRAL & WESTERN BANK", it said, and:

"CASHCARD RECEIPT.

WITHDRAWAL £90.00

BALANCE £22.76.

HELLO JAYNE. LONG TIME NO SEE.

REMEMBER MY EYES IN TORQUAY?

THANK YOU FOR USING CENTRAL & WESTERN CASHCARD."

Jayne shook her head slowly. "But who would do such a thing?"

"Somebody's obviously got a weird sense of humour at that bank." He tossed the small white square of paper onto the table. "I'm sure it's nothing to worry about."

She picked up the remote control and zapped on a holiday programme. "If I have time tomorrow I'll call in and see them about it. I don't mind someone having a joke, but using my name is a bit much."

"Maybe there's someone at the bank with your name and it was meant for... What's the matter? You look like you've seen a ghost."

She didn't hear him. "That's Torquay," she murmured at the television.

At 9.30 Alex was playing squash and Jayne was alone in the house. The novel she was reading was becoming out of focus so she turned off the bedside lamp. Within three minutes she was asleep.

For the first time in over a year she dreamed about the accident. Brian turned away from the cash machine, and as he walked into the road he suddenly remembered the cashcard and turned back, unaware of the car, and her dream-eyes closed in anticipation of the impact which in reality she hadn't witnessed. When she re-opened them her stomach plummeted to her knees as the rollercoaster she found herself on dipped into a bend. She immediately recognised the surroundings. The clear blue sky was thrown around her head. She screamed silently. Finally she stumbled off to find herself in front of a shop in a pedestrian precinct.

She heard Brian's voice, "Let's see what they say."

She looked up at the shop sign and then at Brian.

(Back in her bedroom, Jayne muttered, over and over, "Allergic to protein.")

The sign read "Atkinson's Opticians." This and Brian's blood-shot eyes gradually permeated her consciousness and she awoke, clutching the sweat-stained sheets.

Four years ago on holiday in Torquay with Brian, he had been told by an optician that he had developed an allergy to de-proteinising tablets and would have to start wearing spectacles. It seemed unlikely to her that anyone he knew at the time would remember something so trivial and, even if they did, that they also worked at the Central & Western Bank.

Wanting to escape the suffocating darkness she clambered out of bed and out onto the landing, turning on the light, and walked unsteadily downstairs. As the kitchen striplight spluttered into life she poured herself a glass of water. She stepped into the lounge and turned on the television, needing contact with civilisation.

Five minutes into the subtitled film she had forced herself to watch, a splash of white in the wastepaper basket vied for attention like an itch in the corner of her eye. She got up, meaning to push the scrap of paper back out of sight but instead picking it up and unrolling it.

"HELLO JAYNE," it still said.

Moments later she found herself getting dressed, grabbing the car keys and heading for the front door.

He believed that it was thinking about Jayne that had kept him from going mad. Sometimes he yearned for her, for a release from the intolerable loneliness. Sometimes he cursed her, for putting him in this situation with her impatience. He could picture her on the other side of the road, glancing at her watch.

"All right, all right," he had muttered, grabbing the coughed-up money and stuffing it into his wallet. He was aware of the car, and he was confident it would miss him. He was more conscious of Jayne's mouthed "Hurry up." When the machine bleeped he made the mistake of turning round. Solid metal collided with soft flesh. The pain filled up his body, blood cell by blood cell.

Understandably, it all went hazy.

It was as though his spiritual self had carried on to the bank on auto-pilot. Of course, his hand passed right through when he grabbed for the card. There were screams behind him. He didn't look. Didn't want to or didn't have time. Did a shove from unseen hands send him through the front of the bank? All he knew was that the blackness engulfed him, a blackness that would be relieved by the occasional flash of light which made his body, spiritual or not, spasm briefly. In that timeless void it may have taken him six days or six years to figure out that the flash was caused by someone using the cash machine.

He had always heard voices. After the initial doubts about his sanity he realised it was people he heard, standing in front of the bank. He started to believe he might end his isolation by utilising that thread-like connection with the real world.

His first reaction was to shout for help. He heard his voice, but he had a feeling it was only in his head. He tried again. When he heard raised voices he concentrated and could make out words.

"What's that on the screen?"

"Some idiot's messing about."

"There's something on the printout as well. Looks like "Help me." What're they playing at?"

That was the first breakthrough. The second came when he noticed the tiniest flash of light as somebody in the real world retrieved their card. He thought perhaps it was static from their hand. He was certain that he felt it, too.

He waited. And hoped. His anger at Jayne and his longing for her bubbled under the surface of his disembodied mind.

By 10.30 she had pulled up outside the bank and was plucking up the courage to get it over with. She had to convince herself she wasn't losing her mind.

The clock on the dashboard ticked over to 10.45. She knew she had to come to a decision for Alex would be home soon. She took out the cashcard and strode over the road to the cash machine.

She inserted the card, keyed in the code number and breathed in again, the musty night air rattling in her nostrils. Her heart reverberated in her ears like distant gunfire. The troops edged closer when green words flickered onto the black screen. They retreated slightly as she smiled weakly at their familiarity:

CASH WITHDRAWAL.

BALANCE

STATEMENT

OTHER OPTIONS

RETURN CARD.

Jayne stood there, soaking up the sight before her which was comforting and real. She would get home now before Alex did. Brian's death was obviously preying on her mind again. She would try to get some sleep, even if she had to take Valium for the first time in a while.

She moved her hand towards the keypad. The screen flickered and she looked up, wide-eyed.

"HELLO JAYNE."

A scream was trapped in her straw-lined throat. She backed away, intending to bolt for the car.

"PLEASE DON'T BE SCARED. IT'S ONLY ME."

She had no idea why the words stopped her. A car sailed past, just behind her yet a hundred miles away. The words blinked off.

"IT'S BRIAN. I CAN SEE YOU."

The word 'how' formed itself on her lips.

"I DON'T KNOW HOW. BUT I STILL LOVE YOU, JAYNE."

That's it, she thought, I've finally gone over the edge.

The screen went blank. She was welded to the spot by both uncertainty and fear. A minute passed. She could feel Brian's presence. She could hear her own breathing, heavy and laboured. She could hear his, deep and whispering. She leaned forward, half-consciously intending to retrieve the card.

"DO YOU STILL LOVE ME?"

This time she did run to the car.

Before inserting the ignition key Jayne realised she would have to go back. Her 'sensible' half told her it was to fetch the card. Her other half knew better.

She got out of the car and walked across the road. For the last time she stood in front of the cash machine. She didn't notice that her heart was thundering against her chest, only that it was aching.

"THANK GOD YOU'RE BACK. I THOUGHT I'D SCARED YOU OFF FOR GOOD."

"No, Brian, " she heard herself say.

The screen went blank. In her mind's eye Jayne saw Brian's face, fixed in contemplation. She heard his breathing, breaking the delicate surface of the night: submerging, resurfacing, submerging, resurfacing.

"DO YOU STILL LOVE ME?" The words weren't green on black, they were his voice - familiar sounds in her ears.

A tear swelled in the corner of her eye like a tiny diamond. "Yes," she murmured. The diamond burst and released a fine line of water down her cheek.

"DO YOU WANT US TO BE TOGETHER AGAIN?" His voice, low and barely audible, touched at her heart, easing the pain slightly.

She nodded slowly. She heard her 'sensible' half say, "How can we when you're..." The word caught in her throat.

"DEAD? NOT EXACTLY. MORE SORT OF "IN LIMBO."" His voice was clearer again: **"BUT WE CAN BE TOGETHER AGAIN."**

For a few moments he said nothing. To Jayne the whole world was the screen and the space she occupied.

"I NEED YOU JAYNE."

She didn't notice she had bitten her lip until she drew blood.

"PUT YOUR HAND ON THE SCREEN – MAYBE I CAN TOUCH YOU."

She sensed his sorrow. Her hand edged towards the screen. It was a millimetre away when she felt tiny tendrils caressing the nerves beneath her palm. "Together," she said softly. She closed her eyes. She saw his arm outstretched, his palm touching hers. **"IN LIMBO,"** he said in her memory. His breath became the stirring of a breeze and disappeared into the darkness.

"No! " she yelled. Her hand was glued to the screen. She felt nauseous. Stars flickered at the rims of her eyes. She pulled up her left hand and yanked at her right arm with all her strength. There was a crackle of electricity and she fell backwards.

She scrambled to her feet and grabbed at the cashcard which had reappeared, vaguely aware that she shouldn't leave it there. She pulled her hand away quickly - it was white-hot. As she backed away a receipt was spat out at her. She picked it up and turned round.

She had to get away. This was too much to take. One foot had dropped into the yawning chasm of madness: she had to pull it back out.

She stumbled into the road. Halfway across she became conscious of a carhorn, anxious and deafening. She looked up into the shocked eyes of the driver. Brakes squealed. There was a rush of air, the stench of exhaust

fumes...

...and she threw herself at her car door, scrabbling for the handle.

She couldn't remember getting into her car. She couldn't remember what the driver had shouted when he appeared at the window. The drive home was a blur.

Alex smiled to himself at Jayne's forgetfulness. He pulled into the High Street and slowed down as he approached the bank.

"I don't believe it," Jayne had said ten minutes earlier as she looked up at him with sleep-laden eyes.

He sat down on the bed and stroked her hair. "What's the matter?"

She sat up. "I left my card in the cash machine."

She started to get out of bed. "It's all right," he said, rattling his car keys at her, "I'll go. You go back to sleep." He kissed her on the cheek and she thanked him and pulled the quilt back up to her face.

He got out of the car, taking care to lock it because his wallet was on the dashboard. He crossed the road to the bank. He was so amazed that the cashcard was still in the machine that he didn't notice there was no bleeping to accompany the words **"PLEASE TAKE CARD"** on the screen. He leaned forward, hand outstretched.

Jayne had left the light on and was dozing when she heard the front door rattle open. She heard footsteps, slow and careful, on the stairs. She sat up. The photograph of Brian on the beach in Torquay lay on Alex's pillow. She hurriedly pushed it under her own pillow.

The bedroom door creaked open. Alex stood there, a strange expression on his face. He seemed to be studying the room. His eyes caught hers and her mouth was suddenly very dry.

"Long time no see," he said, and he walked slowly over. "Actually, it's great to see without glasses again." Something rustled under his foot. He stooped down and picked up a small square of paper:

"CENTRAL & WESTERN BANK

CASHCARD RECEIPT.

SEND SOMEONE ELSE.

THEN WE CAN BE TOGETHER AGAIN."

©Sean Jeffery

Memories

by

B. Gerad O'Brien

B. Gerad O'Brien

Born in 1947 in Tralee, Ireland, Gerad has lived for the last 25 years in Newport, South Wales with his wife Jennifer and two daughters, Shelly and Sarah.

After a hard day at work as a supermarket manager in Cardiff he finds writing short stories not only great fun but also immensely therapeutic.

His love of words was kindled as a child by listening to the stories of John B Keane and Bryan MacMahon who he often met whilst spending summer holidays in Listowel with his uncle Moss Scanlon, whose harnessmakers shop was a magnet for all sorts of colourful characters.

Memories

by

B. Gerad O'Brien

It was strange seeing the old Picturedrome again. After 25 years I don't know what I expected. But I never thought that it would be exactly as I remembered it.

A gust of wind threw the rain against me and it peppered the door with droplets, and somewhere in the dark clouds that rolled across the late Summer sky the thunder grumbled.

On impulse I tried the handle, and to my amazement it gave a click and the door creaked open.

A streak of lightening lit up the huge foyer as I poked my head inside, and the familiar smell of the place wafted over me. Suddenly it was as if I was a kid again.

There used to be three Cinemas in the town back then. But the Picturedrome was special. It was there that I had my first summer job.

I wallowed in the memories as I walked up the steps to the doors with the 'Way In' sign above them. I could still see Bridie Maguire standing there, taking the tickets and tearing them in half, her beautiful green eyes sparkling with the importance of it all.

I gave the door a push and looked inside, then I walked down into the huge auditorium. The stage curtains were open, revealing the enormous silver screen that once attracted us like flies on a Saturday afternoon, and for a brief second I thought I saw it flicker again.

Technically my job had been to go around town sticking up the posters, but I also had to collect the films from the Railway Station. I didn't mind because it gave me the opportunity to help Bridie's father up in the Projection Box.

I spend hours assisting Danny, rewinding the spools and lacing up the projectors as he drank endless cups of tea which he brewed on an old paraffin stove. In return he'd let me watch the film through the tiny viewing window.

"Can I help you?"

I spun around.

The grey haired man stared at me intently.

"Oh, I.."

Suddenly in the faint light something about his features triggered a memory.

"Danny? Danny Maguire?"

He blinked a few times.

"Yes?"

"Good grief!" I laughed. "After all these years. I don't believe it. But I don't expect you remember me. It must be 25 years or more. I was just a kid."

"Sure, I remember you." He patted me on the arm. "How could I ever forget that mop of red hair? Liam, isn't it?"

"You remember me?"

"Of course I do." He looked me up and down. "Didn't you have tiny legs in those days, they could never reach the ground when you got up on that bike."

"That's right." I laughed. "I remember that. And I fell off it more times than I stayed on."

"And what about the time they put up the notices that Bill Posters Will Be Prosecuted." He was chuckling now. "We told the cops that your name was Bill Posters. When the Sergeant came in you hid under the stool in the ticket office. He only wanted a ticket for Oklahoma!"

Danny threw back his head and gave a huge bellow.

"But what about you?" I asked. " I never thought I'd see you here after all this time. How are you?"

"I'm grand, sure." He straightened his tie. "Grand altogether."

"The place doesn't look any different." I glanced around at the rows of seats that swept down in front of me. "I can't believe it, even the smell."

"And what about yourself? Where've you been all this time?"

"Well," I sat on the arm of a seat. "When my Dad lost his job we went to America. I joined the Navy. I did twenty one years. I thought I'd come home and see if any of my folks were still around."

"You haven't been home for twenty one years?"

"Well, I always intended to come back, but..."

He nodded.

"Look," he waved towards the stairs. "I was just going up to the Box. Come on up and I'll make you a cup of tea." He suddenly stopped. "But you don't like tea, though. You always wanted that Coke stuff. Well, I didn't have any then, and I haven't got any now."

He chuckled, then he took off up the stairs. Something bothered me about the way he trotted up the winding staircase. There was something not quiet right. But he seemed fit enough. The same old Danny. The same old grey cardigan.

"How's Bridie these days?" I shouted after him.

"Did you know she was chosen for that ice cream advertisement?" He said over his shoulder. "Her picture was in the papers, smiling and holding up an ice cream cone."

"Yes," I said. "I remember that."

"They still haven't paid her, you know!" He said softly. "But I expect that's how it is in business, always pay at the last possible moment."

"What...?"

I knew I was frowning. His eyes twinkled, but there was no humour in them.

Up in the Box he rattled around, putting the films back in their cases.

"These aren't the same old projectors?" I said, rubbing my hand along the cold grey metal.

"What? Now, there's nothing wrong with these beauties." He patted one of them. "They're the best in the world. Now, what about that tea?"

He shuffled over to the small paraffin stove on the table and turned up the wick, then he cracked a match and lit it. He turned the control on the side until the flame became an intense blue, then he put the old kettle on to boil.

"Yes, my Bridie is turning into a fine young lady, so she is."

He wiped his hands on an old tea towel.

I began to feel uneasy. It was as if I'd wandered through a sort of time warp. Something was making me feel very uncomfortable.

Outside the thunder cracked and a flash of lightening zipped overhead, and a sudden breeze blew into the Box and it caused the newspaper on the table to flutter. At the same time the flame from the paraffin heater danced wildly and it seemed to snake out deliberately towards the edge of the paper. The paper touched the flame for the briefest of moments, but it was enough. The corner blackened instantly and curled away and the flame spread across it in the blink of an eye.

Danny Maguire leapt towards the table and grabbed the newspaper, trying to stop it being totally engulfed, but the flame scorched his hand and he dropped it onto the floor. The pages spread apart and flew off in different directions, one of them curling around the base of the projector.

Danny's awkward scramble caused the heater to wobble, and it flipped onto its side sending a shower of paraffin out over the fallen paper. By the time it hit the floor it had already ignited, and the flames spread with a woosh across the floor and up the side of the projector.

I grabbed Danny and pulled him across the Box to the door, and we reached it just as the flames shot up the wall and across the dusty ceiling.

"Fire," Danny screamed. "Fire. Help. Get some water. For God's sake get some water."

He pulled the fire bucket off the nail on the wall and he threw the water into the seat of the fire, but it didn't even cause a splash.

"Don't panic." I shouted. "Get down the stairs. We can call the Fire Brigade from there."

I grabbed his arm and pulled him away. The fire had now spread to the outside of the door and the white hot flames snaked towards the long heavy curtains that hung down the wall at the back of the stairs. And with unbelievable speed it flashed up the heavy fabric and hit the ceiling before it curled back down to reach the bottom of the stairs before us.

"Come on!" I was screaming as I pulled Danny through the fierce heat that was sucking at us from every angle.

Suddenly he stopped dead and he turned violently, and he almost knocked me off of my feet.

"Bridie!" He yelled. "My Bridie's still up in the office."

"What office?"

I had never seen an office up there.

"The top office." He cried. "She's sorting the money. She banks the money every Tuesday."

I grabbed at his cardigan and pulled him back.

"You can't go back up there, you fool. You'll get killed."

But he fought like someone possessed and he wriggled out of the cardigan, then he ran back up the steps before I could stop him. And his voice echoed desperately as he disappeared into the thick wall of flame that was now all around us.

There was no way that I could follow him. The flames were now out of control and moving too fast, and the heat was already starting to blister my face and hands. So in desperation I wrapped the cardigan around my head and I threw myself down the rest of the stairs, and I slammed into the front door.

Frantically I searched for the handles and yanked them open, and I staggered out into the clean damp air.

At that very moment the clouds parted and the rain stopped, and a beam on sunlight touched the pavement causing little wisps of steam to rise. And the young policeman jumped out of his skin when I touched him on the shoulder.

"Good God!" His face reddened. "Where did you come from?"

"The Picturedrome...a fire!"

He gave a relieved smile and took off his cap.

"Well, that's funny." He said. "Wasn't our old Sergeant telling us about that this very morning. He remembers it well.."

"What? A fire in the cinema?"

"Well, it was a cinema alright, about twenty years ago." He continued. "But it seems the place burned down one wet afternoon for no apparent reason. They thought that one of the projectors caught fire. The poor old operator and his daughter were trapped in there."

"Twenty years ago...?"

"About that, yes."

I turned and gave the big doors a mighty shove. They were locked solid.

"You won't open them." He laughed. "They're only for show. A relic, so to speak. There's a solid wall behind them. The place was turned into a car park for the Council years ago. Still," He put his cap back on and sauntered away, "Not many people go to the pictures these days, anyway."

I watched him walk away, then I turned and picked up the old grey cardigan that I had dropped beside the big green doors.

©B Gerad O'Brien

Premonition

Imagination?

Clocking In

Three Short Stories

by

Linda Lawrie

Linda Lawrie

Born and educated in Oxford. Anyone who remembers Cowley St John when it was split by the Cowley Road, put your hand up. Such long memories! Poor old souls!

Served time honoured apprenticeship on leaving school as GPO telephonist, which, when combined with self-taught typing skills, stood her in good stead for a variety of administrative positions for; solicitors; builders; hauliers; seed brokers; estate agents; you name a firm or company and she has probably 'temped' there!

Currently she is working part-time enabling her greater flexibility towards her writing career.

Her hobbies are reading, crosswords, wildlife and pestering literary agents and publishers.

Premonition

by

Linda Lawrie

The cool summer breeze whipped at the loose ends of her long hair as the engine responded to the twist of throttle. The slightly louder purr made music in her ears.

She felt good to be out on the open road. The weather was perfect, the road surface for once, smooth and Sue was thoroughly enjoying riding nowhere in particular. This was what having your own bike meant - enjoyment - being out and about just for the sheer pleasure it gave, going where you liked and not caring. A most glorious feeling of freedom and every moment was to be cherished.

Leaning into a corner, Sue could see a speck at the side of the road in the distance which became a person as she closed in on the spot. Much nearer now, she could make out a leather clad form, helmet dangling from one hand, thumb hopefully extended. A hiker. Should she stop? Yes, why not, nothing would spoil this wonderful day and it just might be the start of a good ride out.

Easing forward with her right hand, the left gently drawing on the clutch in unison with her booted foot on the brake, Sue halted just beyond the figure.

For a hitcher he appeared to be in no particular hurry or maybe he was taking in the striking, leather clad figure before him. She hoped so because she was giving him the once-over! "Not at all bad either!" She thought, although it was a pity about his full face helmet, it would cover his good looks!

Helmets were the one thing she didn't like about biking gear and wore an open face one. This appraisal of each other took the mere six strides he made to reach her machine.

"Hi."

"Hi yourself." She smiled.

"Can you take me to the nearest garage?"

Sue barely hid her disappointment but out loud said. "Sure, what's happened to your bike?" Instead of the 'Oh is that all.' that was on the tip of her tongue.

With little other reaction to her friendliness, his reply came short and muffled. "Had to leave it behind."

Watching him strap the helmet into place, Sue studied its unusual pattern of green stripes, entwining their path from a point near the visor to the rear edge.

His reluctance to talk was puzzling. Usually bikers were a friendly lot and were only too pleased to chat with anyone showing any interest at all, let alone a fellow rider and enthusiast.

She could hardly feel his weight on the back as he positioned himself behind her, he was used to riding pillion then, good, she should have no problems with controlling the bike when cornering. It would be a short trip to the garage, hardly time to get to know the lad but maybe he would need a lift on to somewhere else or back along this road after he'd finished.

Peering into her mirror part way there to look at her passenger, Sue's naturally warm smile froze in place. The shock and horror of the sight made her lose control temporarily for a moment, the bike swerved violently and she was thankful for the early hour and quietness of the road.

The helmet, now missing, had been replaced by her passenger's face which had become a skull!

She skidded to a halt on the forecourt of the garage, back tyre locked, in her frenzy to escape the visage. Sue jumped off the bike, automatically kicking at the prop stand, leaving the engine running and fled for safety into the garage itself.

Peeping cautiously back round the workshop door, she could not see her passenger anywhere. The area, the street totally empty!

Linda Lawrie

With heart pounding, Sue woke, hands clenched in tight clammy fists, a scream frozen in her throat, a weak groan took its place at her lips. She tried desperately to dispel the feeling of latent dread. It was some time before she could face moving let alone the process of completely leaving the bed.

The shower eased away the last of her tension. Sue hummed happily as she got dressed. Breakfast ready, the dream was all but forgotten. The day ahead held too many pleasures for her to retain that bit of garbled rubbish for long. She was to meet up with her friends this morning and they would go out for a day's ride somewhere.

The sun shone obligingly, the birds sung, all was well. "What a wonderful time we'll have." Sue thought as she zipped up her leathers. She could picture them all on the beach, splashing in the water, sunbathing, talking and laughing.

He'd been waiting on the side of the road for what felt like an age. "Does nothing come along here?" "Does no-one get up early?" Frustration at wasting so much of a beautiful day gnawed at his insides. He longed to be out and about not sat around in hopes of catching a lift.

"If only." He sighed.

If only he'd got up earlier. If only his bike hadn't refused to start. If only he hadn't promised to meet the other enthusiasts, also hoping for a great day out!

Dave had met the friendly group a few nights before and happily accepted their invitation to join with them when the suggestion of a ride came up. It was not easy being new to an area and they had made him feel welcome.

"And now I'm going to let them down."

He sighed once more, settling his chin into cupped hands, elbows resting on knees.

Sue wheeled her Yamaha out of the garage and on to the road before starting it up. Funny how parents could be woken by that really rather gentle sound and yet snore through a persistent and shrill bedside alarm during the week!

Having already walked quite a way, Dave was reluctant to go further. It was better than doing nothing though, so he unkinked his legs from their cramped crouching position and made to move on. He would continue to the meeting point even if it did mean arriving well after the others had left. It was too nice a day to go nowhere at all.

He stopped within a couple of strides and cocked his head to one side. 'I don't believe it! The sound of an engine, a motorcycle at that.' He thought out loud as he hurriedly struck what he hoped to be the 'right' pose. His thumb stuck well out, helmet dangling from his right hand in the long grass.

The cool summer breeze whipped at the loose ends of her long hair as the engine responded to the twist of throttle. The slightly louder purr made music in her ears. It was going to be a beautiful day.

Leaning into a corner, Sue could see a speck at the side of the road in the distance which became a person as she closed in on the spot. Much nearer now, she could make out a leather clad form, helmet dangling from one hand, thumb hopefully extended. A hiker.

She could feel the blood in her veins chilling as her heart strained to pump it round her veins.

"Oh God, Nooo." Her mind screeched.

The dream!

It was coming back to her slowly but surely!

She had been through this before.

Yes!

The speck was a man hitching a ride. 'Not with me, buddy.' Sue wasn't going to risk it for real. Despite telling herself how silly she was being she turned on the power and screamed straight passed the startled figure.

Dave only caught a glimpse of her terrified face as she flashed passed him, throttle nearly wide open. He had no chance to further consider the passing machine and rider as another bike could be heard in the distance.

The group were gathered all but for Pete. Sue was on edge still and just saying. "..then I saw his helmet, black with intertwined green lines..." She froze as Pete arrived, Dave in tow. Suddenly the day was turning sour on her. Dave was saying. "..the look on her face, God, man, it was somethin'. Horrified, that is the only way to describe her expression! Wouldn't have noticed but for the open helmet she wore, unusual enough in itself these days." He continued.

The two of them stood stock still staring on recognising each other. Sue's audience rapt in her story continued to watch her intently. It was Pete who broke the spell.

"Hey, Sue, what's up?"

"It's a long story, tell you another time."

Sue was very reluctant to say anything at all in front of this Dave person.

Dave strolled to join the rest. A sudden babble of voices started up at once, with everyone eager to get things back to normal. More than once Sue was caught staring at Dave's helmet or looking oddly at his face.

"You expecting him to sprout horns or what?" Someone joked. There was no answering smile from Sue.

To prove all was well - to the others as well as herself - Sue offered to carry Dave pillion on their journey to the beach, despite still feeling uneasy about the whole thing.

The temptation to peer in her mirror to see Dave's face was too strong to resist, she was back with her dream and expected a skeleton to return her look at any moment!

It didn't, Dave smiled back at her each time. A warm, friendly smile that reassures. The sort of smile you always hope a boy will give you when you have met for the first time and fancy him like crazy. Only she didn't, not yet. Inwardly Sue began to regret her earlier foolish reactions to him.

Each time she turned her full attention back to the road though, a cold tingle ran across her shoulders and down her spine.

With a twist of the throttle for a last burst of speed on the remaining open road, still calling herself a silly bitch - for Dave seemed a nice enough guy really - Sue gave one final glance in the mirror; this time to check for any stragglers.

That, was when her passenger's face did reflect as a skull, a mere instant before the air echoed with metallic sounds of the impact as a truck reversed directly into their path.

©Linda Lawrie

Imagination?

by

Linda Lawrie

L ate evening. Shadows are cast by the glow of the gas lamps that line the walls. Scary enough for a seven year old but made worse by her having to pass that painting.

The one at the foot of the long staircase, you must recall from your earlier visit the one I mean. In a darkened room a small group of seated people, their outspread hands resting on a table, finger tips just touching. The once bright colours have faded over the years. This does not detract from the atmosphere the artist has built into it with his brush strokes.

The background is very dark indeed.

This is what an imaginative seven years reacts to. The dark. What lurks at the back of that picture?

You and I would say "nothing, it is simply a painting."

Annabel's parents have chided her often for being 'so silly' about the whole thing. Frequent enough for her not to mention it any more.

Being the 'big girl' she now is at such an advanced age, she keeps her fears to herself. Doesn't even tell Nanny how she trembles just being near it. How, at night, on going to her room, she runs passed the spot, not stopping on the stairs until she turns right at the top and reaches the safety of the passage in which lies her room.

This night is different. Her father is returned from his travels. Annabel is permitted to stay up and greet him - on the promise she will go straight to her room afterward.

This done, with her father beside her at the foot of the stairs, Annabel does not so much as glance at the dreaded picture. For once, happily she mounts the steps, holding on to the solid carved handrail and pauses to blow her father one last kiss from the top before turning off the stairway.

Settled into bed, excitement at her father's homecoming keeps Annabel from sleeping. She imagines all the wonderful things that will happen on the approach to Christmas, now that he's here.

She hears a noise, in anticipation of a visitor to her room, she softly leaves her bed and moves across the room in order to greet them, lips puckered ready for a quick and final goodnight kiss, Annabel opens the door.

The corridors is empty. A slight but icy breeze tugs gently at her night-gown, Annabel shivers, she clutches the neckline tighter to her.

At the far end of the corridor, silhouetted and shadowed by the pale glow of the gas lamps, Annabel sees a shape climbing out of the window. Believing it to be one of the servants secretly leaving the house - it is a constant amazement to one so young what antics a servant will get up to! - she runs back across to her own window to try and see who it is.

Clouds part, the moon's light is strong as the shape - obviously no servant - scurries over the lawn, heading toward the wood in the distance. It pauses briefly by the oak tree, yes it still stands, and looks up.

This long haired, black gangly-limbed being with misshapen head and bright, deep red eyes, looks for a few seconds at the building then continues its scurry to unknown haunts.

Annabel's screams in the early hours of the morning, before the day casts the night's cloudy mantle bring a concerned but rather cross Nanny to her bedside. She was becoming a problem child after all. Nanny thought it had been too good to be true, that this girl could not be the easiest charge she had ever known, giving not a moment's serious worry.

The layout of the house and grounds may be familiar to you on your next visit, but do stop a moment, pay attention to the painting at the foot of the staircase. Something has changed since you last saw it. Since I looked at it even.

Those people seated so serenely around the table, if you look closely, the fingers of their outspread hands no longer touch.

The background does not appear to be quite so dark as it used to be, the colours are a little more vibrant.

Maybe someone has had it cleaned?

Annabel no longer fears the picture, no longer thinks twice of passing it. Her nightmare has never recurred.

Not since the night of her dream.

©Linda Lawrie

Clocking In

by

Linda Lawrie

I was at a loose end. Which made it an ideal chance to visit my best friend Jennifer. She sounded rather excitable when I telephoned. In fact she had been on the point of ringing me to suggest I go round that very morning for coffee.

The cups and plates had scarcely been laid when she plunged into her tale without preamble.

Jennifer began.

"I was alone in the house. Because it was a miserably damp, dull day, I restlessly drifted through the rooms, searching for something to do until Mark came home, finally deciding on a quiet read.

For the umpteenth time, before settling down, I looked at the clock. Time was dragging. Then I thought it might look better in the opposite alcove and changed it over with a vase. I stood back to see the effect, replaced the vase, tried the clock again. I just couldn't make up my mind! Leaving the clock in its new place, I snuggled into the chair and started to read in the peace and quiet."

That was Jenny, always re-arranging things!

"The voice came indistinctly. To begin with, I didn't even think it was a voice. Then a little clearer came.

"You've done it again!"

I looked up, no-one there – I went back to my book, puzzled.

"How did you do that, lass?"

It was much clearer this time, something not to be ignored, nor did it want to be. Without really thinking and before I could stop myself, the reply, "Do what?" came from my lips.

"That's twice you've perched the clock in mid air!"

"Whaat?!"

This was silly. Not only did I hear a disembodied voice but I talked back to it.

"What are you doing in my parlour anyway?"

"Your parlour? This is my living room!"

Matters were worsening, I now argued!

"Ah, you're becoming clearer."

As the voice stated this, I began to make out the vague shape of a man. Minutes passed in silence. Surely I had fallen asleep, this was a dream. I rubbed my eyes, he didn't vanish.

He turned as though his attention was attracted by someone behind him, then turned and faced me again. By now he was quite clear and I seemed to be to him for, he said.

"Excuse my behaviour but I must learn more of you, particularly as you dress in a most peculiar way - if you forgive my saying so, not at all lady-like."

I looked down at my jogging pants and sweat shirt, nothing so odd about them really, then looked a little more carefully at him.

"Your own clothes look very different too." I responded.

"I have just come home from work." He explained.

Home from work at 1.45 pm?

In a brief but thorough study I mentally noted the differences between us. From his clothes I guessed he worked hard. Probably, a labourer of some sort. Again it appeared he was talking to someone else, so I asked.

"Do you have another person there - I cannot see them?"

"My wife. She thinks I've got the D.T.'s as she can't hear, let alone see you herself!"

We laughed at this together. Anticipating my question Jennifer said.

"We accepted the situation like an every day occurrence, that was the incredible thing. Why I don't know but it seemed so natural and right."

She hurriedly continued with her story. The look on her face ordered no further interruption.

"The clock became the main topic of our conversation. Obviously by moving it I'd triggered off a reaction of some kind. We talked about possibilities of what could have happened but came to no real conclusion. The suggestion of removing the clock and then replacing it to see if it 'worked' again was strongly rejected by my 'visitor', he feared the experiment would fail and didn't want to risk that. Nor did he move far from the spot where he stood, in case it 'broke the spell', even though he was talking to me from the corner of the chimney breast!

He remarked that changes had been made to the house in that case as he certainly was not stood up against the chimney breast.

Then he faded out a little, only to reappear again, seated. It would seem his wife had said if he insisted on talking to himself for hours on end, he might as well be comfy. Bringing over the chair had distorted the 'picture' but not actually destroyed it altogether.

He offered me a seat too, which I declined. I hadn't the nerve to try out his offer of hospitality - what if I became stuck there? Goodness knows where - and when. No my bravery didn't extend that far!

He looked as though he was making his mind up whether to say something or not.

"That clock." He suddenly said, thoughtfully. *"How did you get it, when we've got it here?"*

Good question. It had me stumped. How could it be in two places at once? To each of us it was as real as it was to the other. 'The other' didn't exist and yet, there we were, talking.

I told of how I'd gone to a local sale and bought it because it was so pretty, not as though there'd been any intention of buying a clock, I just hadn't been able to resist it." Explained Jennifer.

His reply to my asking how he'd come by it was much longer and by far more interesting.

He - we never got around to exchanging names - began his story by saying as how, every day on his way back and forth to work at the mill, he stopped outside a shop and gazed at the clock, sat in its place of pride in the centre of the display. Despite his description of the route he took, nothing sounded familiar at all. Anyway, he went on to tell how:

"One day I stood longer than usual, I was close on being late for work, the first time in over thirty years. The Under Manager was waiting, arms folded, face scowling. I thought it was my lot. Especially when he took me to the Manager's office without a word being spoken. There, I learnt the

Foreman had been in an accident, and would have to be laid off. I was made up in his place. It was the answer to my prayers! A rise in salary which meant the clock could be mine, just in time for our anniversary too."

"On the way home that evening, I went in to the shop and lodged a small deposit, promising to return each Friday until the payments were completed. It was a proud and delightful moment when I gave it to my wife, so carefully wrapped."

He paused, then went on;

"My wife was thrilled with it."

So intent on hearing every detail, I failed to notice immediately that he'd stopped speaking and was looking at me in a peculiar way. When I did become aware of this, I asked if all was well. He didn't reply immediately but continued to look intently at me then asked if I'd "come a bit closer", he rose from his chair. I did as he asked but not too near, you understand, despite my boldness up 'til then, I was still very cautious.

We stood for a moment longer then he thanked me politely and we sat back down – a smile was on his face now.

"But of course, you must remember this quite well, after all the patience you showed."

Now I was thoroughly startled, and not a little scared – he said it with such conviction. This was becoming eerie.

"What do you mean by that?" I asked.

In a surprised voice he asked further.

"Don't you remember the pleasure we both felt the day of the final payment? You signed the receipt with a flourish."

Through my trembling somehow I got to my feet, apologised and moved the clock back to its original place. My visitor could no longer be heard or seen. Shivering, I sat back down. When I'd calmed down I looked at the clock again. Surely Mark should be home soon?

It must have stopped. A mere five minutes only, had passed since I opened my book and yet so much had happened – it wasn't possible – but it had taken place! As the full enormity hit me, I shook even more.

Predictably, Mark didn't believe a word of what I told him. But did have the grace to try placing the clock in the other alcove – nothing, no voice, no man. I didn't know whether to be thankful or not, after all Mark remained sceptical."

The coffee and cakes had long since disappeared. We sat in silence.

That was Jennifer's story, the cause of her agitation. Even I had my doubts about it - had she fallen asleep and dreamed it all?

The clock had refused to work properly from that day on.

I could only guess at the distress this experience had caused her. Even now, a few days later, in the reliving, her face reflected some of the fear she must've felt at the time.

I stood, went over to the clock and ran my fingers over it lightly. Jennifer begged me not to do as Mark had done and try to recreate the scene. I promised although the temptation was there. I admired the ornate casing, turning it over to examine it in detail, as I did so it fell from my hands.

No obvious damage had been done I noted as I picked it up. I peered closely at the casing to make sure, its ornate gilt work revealed nothing out of place and yet I had felt something. In the bottom back corner, a piece of - what? I worried at it with a fingernail and a piece of paper emerged.

Jennifer, fretting I was trying quietly to put right a major mishap, came over and stood just behind me, then the paper came out.

Carefully I placed the clock down, reassuring her it was fine, unfolded the paper and blinked - hard. Jennifer tried to peer over my shoulder but I wasn't ready to let her see it - just yet.

It was a receipt made out to M SMITH ESQ totalling £3 12s 5d, dated November 1913 and signed JENNIFER STUBBS - with a flourish.

The Lake

by
Dylan Pugh

Dylan Pugh

Born in 1953, Dylan lives in Melton Mowbray and is married with two adult children. He works as a technical process planner for a joinery company.

He has been writing for much of his life and his first published works were Nature Notes in his local Chapel Newsletter.

His poetry has been published in magazines and anthologies in Britain, Ireland, the United States and Japan and he has also read one of his own poems on Radio 5 Live.

His short stories have been read on BBC Local Radio and published in various magazines. He has also written three novels.

Dylan Plath

The Lake

by

Dylan Pugh

The sun was sliding into a band of cloud over the western hills as he manoeuvred the car through the narrow lanes where he had once played. The high hedgerows seemed to meet in the dusk above, his headlights sweeping through them as though they were tunnel walls. Moths flew like white punctuation marks across the passage of his beams.

At the bottom of the hill he came upon the pub. Gravel scrunched beneath his tyres as he pulled into the car-park; the light flooding from the windows coloured it a rich and welcoming gold. Parking beneath the familiar row of mature beeches, he took an overnight bag from the car, locked the door, and walked across the few yards to the pub.

Things had changed in the years he had been away. He knew already that there was a new landlord, having spoken to him when he phoned to check and book a room. Anyway, John would have been long retired, even if he was still alive.

As he stood at the bar, he looked round. The decor was different; plusher, richer. The new wooden panelling which covered the old brickwork glowed gently in the lights, counterpointed here and there by the glitter of the highly polished brasses and strategically positioned copper warming pans. His reverie was interrupted.

"Yes Sir?"

"Williams, Jim Williams. I telephoned yesterday."

"Oh yes. I'm sorry, we were expecting you earlier. I'm Bill Hislop." He held out a hand. "Was it a bad journey?"

Jim shrugged. He recognised the name from the plate above the front door, and shook the proffered hand.

"No, not really. But I left straight from work, and the rush hour rather caught me out."

"Well, you're here now. Let me show you your room, Mister Williams, and you can freshen up. We'll serve dinner whenever you're ready. Within reason," he grinned. He gestured towards the overnight bag. "Is that all your luggage?"

"Enough for tonight. The rest of my gear is in the car. It'll wait till morning."

Half an hour later, washed, refreshed and feeling rather more comfortable in a clean shirt and sweater, Jim stood looking out of the window. Fringing the pool of light at the front of the pub he could see the green of the trees waving in the breeze. Beyond that was nothing but the still, empty darkness that was the lake. A slight shudder passed up his spine. Drawing the curtains against the night, he turned and left the room.

As he came through the stair door and crossed to the bar, a smile hovered on his lips. Altered though the place was since his last time here, some things never changed. In the bar corner sat Old Tom. Amongst the brand new furniture, he seemed to be enthroned on the same scuffed old stool he had used for years. Jim stood close to him, and ordered a pint of Old Growler.

"Evening, Mister Morris," he said, as he waited for his drink.

Tom looked up at him, and recognition slowly dawned in his watery but still alert old eyes. "Young Jim Williams," he replied. "Fancy seeing you here again."

He held out his right hand, as the landlord had done earlier; but clutched in it was an empty glass. Jim took it from him, ordered a refill, and returned the old man's firm, dry handshake.

"Cheers," he responded, as Jim handed him his fresh drink. After taking a long pull at it he leaned back, sighed with deep satisfaction, and cast a shrewd glance at the younger man.

"What brings you back to this neck of the woods?" He inquired.

"Thought I'd come and see what the fishing was like." Jim replied.

The old man smiled, as though over fond memories. "Aye, lad," he said, "there's some good fat trout in that water. There's rich ground under it." Both fell silent, concentrating on their own thoughts and their beer. Jim found it good, as good as his memories had promised.

"Beer's as good as ever," he remarked, holding up his glass. "At least some things don't change."

Tom grinned. "Aye, Bill keeps a good cellar. Mind you, things change more often than not. In fact, the beer's about the only thing round here that hasn't altered." He leaned forward conspiratorially.

"They tarted this place up for the anglers, started serving fancy food, then about double the price of a pint." He screwed up his face in disgust. "And you'll never believe this," he continued, "but they laid a flippin' carpet in here!" His arm swept across the stone-flagged floor, and he laughed.

"Mind you, they soon took it up again, all them fishermen traipsin' through in muddy waders, droppin' dead fish and whatnot all over the pretty pattern." This time his laugh turned to violent coughing as he choked on his beer.

After more desultory chat about the terrible changes, Jim took his leave of the old man and went into the dining room to eat. By the time he emerged Tom had gone, and Jim himself retired to bed soon after.

The following morning dawned bright and clear. After the kind of breakfast he would never even dream of, let alone cook and eat alone in his flat, Jim strolled along the lakeside. The pub had a private jetty, hidden behind the trees, where a boat was already moored for his use.

He had been provided with a hamper of food and drink, enough to last all day, and loading this, along with transferring his gear from the car to the boat required three journeys. Even so, it was still somewhat short of ten o'clock when he slowly guided the boat out onto the wide waters of the huge lake.

Far from the shore he shipped the oars and, allowing the boat to drift gently with the breeze, sat and gazed at the scenery, over the hills he remembered so well. It was in this valley that he had spent, and lost, his childhood. He looked over the side, but could see little more than a foot below the surface.

Down below him were the rich fields where he had played, the trees he had climbed and fallen out of. He recalled clearly when they had dammed the little river, as he and his friends had done, less successfully, with mud and stones. This huge reservoir had been created for people who lived many miles away, people who had never seen those woods and lanes.

Shaking his head, Jim began to unpack his gear, and prepared to fish.

Time slowly passed. With two fair sized trout lying on a sack in the bottom of the boat, Jim decided to change to coarse gear. After he had cast, he sat, eyes glued to the glowing tip of his float, and allowed his mind to wander as he munched a slice of home made game pie, washing it down with a moderately good wine. Then, from an inner pocket, he took a flask of whisky, hoping it would ward off the freshening breeze.

Whether it was the drink, the hypnotic effect of watching the water, of his memories, or some combination of the three, he fell asleep.

He was woken by a clap of thunder, feeling the vibration rather than hearing it. The sky was black above him, and the first huge drops of rain washed over the lake. He had been lying back, as he had fallen, head and one shoulder over the side of the boat. As he started at the sound, though he half knew what was happening, he was unable to prevent himself from slipping over the side.

Brain blurred from drink and sleep, limbs heavy, he began to flounder in the cold, choppy water. It closed over his head. When he surfaced, the rain was beating into his face. He did not know where the boat was, and slipped beneath the waves again. Striking towards the air, he struggled desperately to remove his heavy coat, and started swimming to where he thought the shore was closest.

The storm blew wilder. His clothing, collecting more water, dragged him down, and he was finding it difficult to breathe. His head dipped below the surface again.

He seemed to see, far below him, treetops, the roofs of cottages; reaching up towards him the spire of a church. Suddenly he longed for peace, for quiet. His struggles weakened. Then, through the roar of the storm, he heard a voice blown on the wind.

"Jim! Hurry up, Jim!" It was a girl's voice, a voice he remembered well.

"Sue!" He tried to call to her, through a mouth filled with water. "Where are you?" He lashed out desperately, weary arms flailing at the rough waves. He could feel the cold seeping into his bones, and wanted to sleep.

"Sue!" He called again.

"Here, Jim! Hurry, over here!" Her voice came loud, clearer now, urgent and commanding. Rain beat at the back of his head. There were lights in his eyes; he saw Sue standing at the cottage door, light falling out around her. He could sense the fear in her voice, tried to reach her, to reassure her.

"Sue, wait! I'm coming!" He swam, feeling nothing of the storm raging about him, hearing nothing but that terrified call. Watching her face, Jim battled against the cold, rolling water.

Bill Hislop and Tom struggled up the path to the back of the pub. Sweating, rain rolling down their faces, they manhandled their burden into the bar, laid it on a bench beneath the steamy, streaked window. Bill went to the phone, called the police, then the doctor.

When he returned, Tom sat on his usual stool. Bill pulled two pints, poured two large whiskies; handed Tom one of each: finally he spoke.

"He was raving when I found him. I went to see whether he was back, what with the storm. Found him on the shore."

"What's he say?"

Bill shrugged. "Some woman's name. Sue, I think." He paused.

"Yes - 'Sue, I'm coming!', that was it. I suppose she is...was his wife. She'll have to be told, I suppose." He fell silent. "Aye, Sue was his wife," Tom muttered, half into his glass. "Wouldn't go with him, she wouldn't. Killed herself, in their cottage, just before they flooded the valley for the reservoir."

He drained his whisky. "Never wanted him to leave either, she didn't."

©Dylan Pugh

Atmospherics

Burying the Hatchet

Two short stories

by
Ashley Stokes

Ashley Stokes

Ashley Stokes was born in Carshalton, Surrey in 1970 and was educated at St Anne's College, Oxford and the University of East Anglia. His writing has been published in Defying Gravity, EM: Music and Writing, This is, "Take 20" and "Hard" a collection of short stories published by the University of East Anglia. He is working on a novel and teaches creative writing at EUA.

Atmospherics

by

Ashley Stokes

"**D**id you hear that? Outside the window. That noise. There it is again, a child crying. Are you awake?"

"No."

"You are."

"I wasn't."

"There it is again. Something is very wrong here."

"Oh get back into bed and come away from that window. It was a bloody cat that's all. A cat wailing on that little roof over the conservatory. Come back to bed and let me go back to sleep . . . Oh you're all cold now. Why did you have to get out of bed?"

"Because I thought . . ."

"I know, I know, just go back to sleep."

"I hate this room. I hate the way that landlady looked at us."

"Then go to sleep. We're leaving first thing."

"I hate this room. It's like when I was ten years old and my grandmother died, and we went round to her little old terraced house to clear out her things. Her room was like this one. Like it hadn't been changed in any way since she first lived in it. It had all the same Edwardian furniture. No electricity. She still had a mangle and a range. And an outside toilet. When she died it was like she'd just seeped into the wallpaper, that it was still there watching you, analysing, judging. It's like that here. Someone died in this room. I can tell. I can feel it. It's in that voice in the wind."

"Cat ... you mean that damn cat in the wind . . ."

"Don't roll over. I'm scared."

"Jesus wept."

"Why did we have to come here? I didn't want to come here. I hate this place. We should've kept on driving. I hate this place. It gives me the creeps."

"It's just a country farm house. It was just a country farm house last year."

"Oh yes. A country farmhouse in the middle of a wood they say is haunted."

"Haunted wood. For fuck's sake."

"It's true. I read it in a book at home. They say this wood's full of old ghosts, that people have disappeared and strange lights have been seen, strange tracks too and no one knows what they are. You know what scared me most? When we were driving up the track here and the headlights were picking out that line of trees by the side of the road that leads up to here and all the leaves were twitching and flickering and brandishing their edges, like they were alive and watching us. And then you turned off the headlights. Don't laugh . . . It wasn't funny. You get a kick out of scaring me don't you?"

"You scare yourself."

"You know I don't like being in the woods at night."

"You were in a car."

"Why do you have to be so facetious?"

"Lack of sleep, perhaps."

"I've always been scared of the woods at night. When I was a student I went on a fruit picking holiday in the south of France. There were about six of us and we stayed at a campsite and walked through some woods and fields to the farm every morning. One evening I met a couple of girls who were also picking fruit. They came from home, though I'd never seen them before. We drank a couple of bottles of wine in a cornfield and watched the sunset. When I finally decided to go back it was dark. As dark as it only gets in the countryside. There was only one thing for it. I had to walk back through the woods. I just stood on the edge at first. All around me, in a huge circle, was rustling and rushing. All I could see were the trunks of the pine trees and great clouds of thick blackness. I thought about going around the wood but it was too big and by this time I was drunk and I wanted to get back as quickly as I could. So I went in. I could hardly see anything. If I looked up I could just about make out the clouds through the treetops. The stench of pine needles began to sting my nose and made me sneeze. And there were sounds. Cooing, shuffling, humming and buzzing. I could feel things crawling on my skin. I was constantly slapping myself for mosquitoes. I didn't even know if I was going in the right direction but I kept moving. Then I reached a clearing. The moon was right above me, a massive full moon ringed with white light. And huge moths were floating up towards it, as if the light drew them like a giant lamp. Strange it was. Moths as big as bats, floating up into the night sky."

"You don't half talk some crap. Moths as big as bats. You're mad you are."

"Don't you want to know if I got back alright. I haven't finished the story."

"You're here, aren't you? Unless I married a ghost. Go to sleep please. I've got to get up and drive in the morning."

"Do you really think I talk crap?"

"What have I heard tonight? Babies crying in the wind. Dead biddies behind wallpaper. The haunted wood. I rest my case, now please . . ."

"Something is wrong. I can feel it."

"Wrong in the head, like you."

"You never listen to me, do you?"

"I'm mercifully absolved that responsibility from midnight to dawn."

"Cheers . . . thanks a lot. Something is wrong here. Do you know who that landlady reminds me of?"

"Norman Bates."

"No . . . I wish you'd listen to me. She reminds me of something I saw when I was little. Well not really little. Twelve or thirteen. We camped out in the garden of someone's parents. I can't remember whose it was now. It was a big house in the old part of town. All the houses were detached and had turrets and great gables. And they all had the most enormous wild gardens, each one like a miniature heath. They were full of statues and rocky ponds and abandoned tree houses and big, sprawling bramble bushes. You could get lost in those gardens. Anyway, we pitched a tent in the garden. The girl whose parents had the garden, her father said "don't worry if you see old Mrs Deasie over the hedge. She's just a bit senile. She mows her lawn in the middle of the night". We all giggled at this, told jokes about it and made up stories, about the old dear next door that no longer knew the difference between night and day.

We stayed out in the tent. It was a great adventure. We had a midnight feast and a pillow fight. We saw hedgehogs and heard owls hooting and foxes screeching. But then, in the middle of the night, are you still listening? . . . we heard the lawn mower, heard it rumbling along in the next door's garden. The dotty old woman was mowing her lawn in the dark and we were desperate to see it.

We grabbed a battery torch and scrambled out of the tent and swept the garden next door with the beam. We couldn't see her at first. The mowing had stopped. We searched the garden again with the torch but still we couldn't find her, until we brought the torch back to right in front of us, right into our garden. She was there, bang in front of us. It was horrible. She was old, like really old, ninety perhaps. She was all white and hairy and warty and she was wearing this filthy night-shirt that was stained with dirt and grass and in her hand she was holding something but the moon glinted off it and at first we couldn't make out what it was.

Then she shook it at us. It was a carving knife. Can you imagine that? A carving knife. We panicked then. Obviously. Had to wake up the parents and get back in. We couldn't stay out in the garden in the dark with her roaming about in whatever state of mind she'd got herself into.

I'll never forget what she looked like, when we caught her in the torch light, the look in her eyes. And that's who that woman that owns this farmhouse reminds me of. That's what disturbs me.

Are you listening?

Are you ...still awake? There's something not quite right here. Look at the way the moonlight throws the shadows of the trees across the ceiling The shadows look like claws. How can they do that? And in the mirror on the wardrobe door you can see us now, lying in this bed with its old-fashioned bedspread. We look strange, contorted . . . Hold me . . . .Please . . . I want you to hold me . . .Oh damn you are asleep now."

"I am holding you."

"You're awake?"

"Of course. What else could I be?"

"Hold me."

"I am."

"You're not. I'm holding on to you. It's not the same. That's better. That's nice."

"Your feet are freezing. I think I'd rather you wore socks. God you're bloody cold. That's the problem with you. Always so bloody cold. Now be quiet and let me sleep. There's nothing wrong here, nothing at all."

Burying the Hatchet

by

Ashley Stokes

The yellow light refracted through rain smears as the sky-scrapers of Frankfurt floated into view. Steve Ganning spotted the Pencil Building, a stake in the heart of the Messe, as his taxi squealed along the autobahn, slashing fins of spray across the tarmac. He never ceased to wonder at the beauty of Frankfurt by night, even though this was his fifteenth bookfair. He'd heard the Germans called it Mainhatten, and he liked this. He even preferred it to New York. There was some-thing more business-like about Frankfurt, and business was his business, that's how he liked to imagine himself. He was the best promotional rights salesman in London, the pillar of Graphex Packages' success. All over the world they were coming to see his product, his books and part-works, his bank of images. He knew it was going to be a great fair.

The cab pulled up outside the Romerberg Hotel, a sleek maze of plate glass and steel struts. Graphex may have skimped on a lot of things, lean and mean as the MD put it, but they looked after the top management. Ganning paid the man, slipping him a machine-neat ten mark note as a tip, and strode into the gleaming reception.

"Ganning's the name, books are the game," he said, over the counter as he booked in. A girl smiled, with efficient sweetness.

His deputy, Miriam was sipping coffee, standing in her pos-tured, limber way. The others were around the stand, making the last presentations of the day to their clients.

"Sorry I'm late," Ganning said, in his gruff, matey voice. "Don't ask about the fucking problems I've had getting here. Never known it so bad. How's it been?"

"Good, good," said Miriam. "A few deals here and there. Cassandra finally closed that Spanish co-edition so that's now in the bag. Howard's been rushing about all over the place."

"Great," said Ganning, though he didn't like Howard. The young man was too prissy, nervy, too thoughtful. He always felt Howard was evaluating him, making secret judgements. He glanced over to the table where Howard was displaying colour spreads to two bearded men. Ganning glowered, clenching his fist. Howard wasn't wearing his jacket. This was against company protocol. No executive must remove his or her jacket on the stand under any circumstance. And he looked glum. Ganning felt like pulling him off the stand there and then and sending him straight back home. Who'd buy anything from someone with a face like that. How many times did he have to tell Howard that a customer buys a sales person not a product. Who'd buy off a man without a jacket and a face like the clap?

Ganning's presence on the stand re-energised the team. They had to impress him or starve and it made Ganning feel powerful, like the captain of a razor-edged frigate, slicing through a sea of profit curves and sales targets. He was going to make a lot of money for the company that week. He could feel it mounting up already. Cassandra's skirt rose up around her thigh as she leaned over her table, running through something with an elderly lady customer. Ganning felt his balls screwing up. He never tried it on with the younger executives. Too risky. Any comeback and his wife might find out. Office flings, dodgy business. Not that this had ever stopped him before but he wasn't going to make the first move with her. The fair had always been a happy hunting ground for Ganning and he was in the mood for an off-duty sale, edgy to score executive stress relief, itchy to hit the flesh-pots of Sachsenhausen. Howard smiled as he came over, flicking his fingers into the signal that meant three sales. Ganning turned his back.

"Hi Steve," said Howard. Ganning made his movements slow

and impregnable, forcing his eyebrows into yellow ridges. "Hi," Howard repeated, waiting for some response. Not getting any, he stared up into Ganning's expressionless eyes. "I made three sales," he said. Ganning blinked. "Three sales. For next August delivery. Forty-five thousand pounds." He waited for Ganning to speak. "Aren't you pleased?" Ganning huffed a deep breath and rose to his full height.

"Listen mate," he growled. "I don't give a monkey's what you've fucking sold today, understand? And I don't want to see you without your fucking jacket on this stand, that's not the way we do things at Graphex, and I don't want to see you moping about when you're with people. If I see as much as a hint of a miserable face, you're fired. Understood?'

Howard's face blackened.

"Yes. Sorry," he said, shyly, and went back to his table.

Ganning said goodbyes and good lucks before swaggering out with a cocky bounce of shoulders. Outside, the rain had slackened to a few clean droplets on the breeze. He lit a cigarette, glancing up at the Pencil Building and its winking lights. Following the deserting crowds, publishing personnel from markets afar, he queued for a ride, eventually clambering into a yellow cab. The driver had a broad moustache and three day stubble that gave him a filthy on-strike look. Nobody would buy from someone who looked like that. Ganning gave clear directions in English with a Teutonic lilt and sat silently in the back, watching the beautiful buildings gliding overhead.

Sachsenhausen was where it all happened, a glass house for one night stands. It had been good to Ganning in the past. As he thumped through a crowded beer cellar he mentally added up the number of times he'd scored at the fair. He reckoned twenty-four in fifteen years and in no season had he failed to confirm orders from at least one eager young thing. His radar was buzzing, blipping around the room as he brushed shoulders at the bar, his jacket done up to conceal his paunch. Too many business lunches had their toll but this didn't stop him selling himself. There were girls, yes, Eurobirds and Americans. He bought a beer and watched the door, perusing the forthcoming titles, assessing their potential in the mumbly rhubarb-rhubarb of conversation. He was aware no one was looking over at him so he enhanced his welcoming, friendly beam. Every girl trusts a smiling man. Every girl wants to fuck a nice, big confident grin.

He spotted three women around a table at the far side. Things looking up, he thought. New possibilities to penetrate the market. One definitely fired his imagination. She was saucy, perhaps about twenty-five. Great tits struggled to escape a silk blouse, their curves traced by slinky pearls. She noticed Ganning was looking at her and smirked beneath playful glances. Play your cards right Steve, he thought, and the dollies will do their dealing.

He drank three glasses of apple cider before the girl's friends got up for the bathroom. She stood erect and surveyed the room. Ganning felt the definite pull of eye contact. Her soft suede shoes seemed to glide along the floor towards him. He readied himself, calculating an opening remark. The first two seconds counted most. A sale is made in the first two seconds, that's when the impression sets in. Her eyelashes fluttered.

"Excuse me mate." Ganning heard a voice from his side. It was an English accent, like a public school boy putting on Cockney. "Can I trouble you for a cigarette?"

Ganning turned. Beside him was a tall, scruffy young man. His face was a sweaty, dark colour and his clothes were like rags. He wore a battered great coat, like something out of a first world war history book. Newspaper peeped from the pockets, bundles of crunched print in some alien alphabet, Greek perhaps. You certainly wouldn't buy anything from him. Ganning took out his duty free B&H's. The stranger took one.

"I couldn't ponce a drink could I, from one Englishman to another?" Ganning briskly rummaged his suit pocket for change and smattered silver and bronze discs across the bar.

"There," he said.

"Cheers mate."

The dirtbag scoured up the change with mole-like scoops for hands. Ganning turned back to the room and stamped his foot, hissing. The girl had evaporated.

Adrian had been watching The Fat Man. He'd been hiding in a shadowy corner, propped up by a short bench. He was annoyed with himself. He'd become careless with funds in Berlin. The last of his money had run out two days before. He'd begged and stolen, a little food, a little coin, stranded in Frankfurt until he could raise enough cash to reach a ferry port. He knew The Fat Man was English. Despite all the time he'd spent in the East he still recognised an Englishman, even in silhouette. He called over the barman with the handlebar moustache and ordered cider in schoolboy German. Slumping against the ridge of the bar, he noticed how aggravated The Fat Man was. His features had sunk into a moroseness like that of a vanquished sportsman. The way he was ignoring Adrian was tangible, in the air like fog.

"Thanks for the drink".

"Don't mention it," Ganning muttered, glumly, without switching his eyes to the dirtbag beside him, the dirtbag that had scuppered his pitch.

"Ex-pat or commercial traveller?" Adrian asked. He thought The Fat Man might be some British banker, serving out a sojourn in Europe's financial powerhouse. Ganning turned on him.

"I was on then and you just fucked it up. I was going to pull that bird."

"Sorry," Adrian said, not wanting to argue. "I didn't realise."

Ganning lit a cigarette, and, noticing a longing look in the dirt-bag's eyes, slid him another with nonchalant grace.

"You at the fair?" he said.

"What fair?"

"The Frankfurt Bookfair."

"No. I'm just passing through. I'm Adrian."

Ganning raised a curious eyebrow.

"Steve Ganning. Sales Director. Graphex." He shook Adrian's hand, regretting the contact afterwards, checking around surreptitiously for any acquaintance, both protective of his image and needing an escape. Steve Ganning was not the sort of man that chatted with tramps. Steve Ganning was a player.

"So you're in books," said Adrian.

"Yeah, I'm in books," Ganning answered. "Have been for nineteen years, since I left school..."

"Do you know the book?" Snapped Adrian, stressing the 'the'.

"What book?"

"The only book."

"What the Bible? Nah, don't do religious stuff. That's all sewn up by other houses, no we do..."

"Not the Bible," said Adrian, slowly, in a way that spooked Ganning. "Dostoyevsky. 'Crime and Punishment'." He flicked his sticky tendril of fringe over his eyes, letting a coil of smoke drift from the corner of his mouth. He never tired of this, this obsession, even though he'd failed. But Ganning had only vaguely heard of Dostoyevsky. He was one of those Russian geezers with a beard. That sort of stuff was tied up by Penguin and the University Presses, especially now you could get classics for a quid. He'd certainly never read it. He only read business books and perhaps a John Grisham or a Terry Pratchett. Books were for selling, not reading.

"No. We do promo books. Cheap, cheerful cookery and craft, with the best colour reproduction and the best prices. Books for the home and that sort of thing."

"It's a great book, you should read it."

There was manic intensity in the dirtbag's eyes. Ganning didn't like intensity. It made people uncomfortable. It was what made him uncomfortable about that ponce Howard. He'd not achieved his dazzling selling record by being intense. He looked around the room for birds and checked his watch. It was still relatively early and later on he'd have a better chance of pulling. The night and the hotel bars would soften them all up for his patter. He decided to humour the dirtbag, pass a little time.

"What's this book about then?" He asked. Adrian sparked forwards, his spindly elbows cracking down onto the bar, retrieving an unoffered cigarette with yellow fingers.

"It's essential," said Adrian. "The only book worth reading. A novel about crime and punishment, crime and aspiration, crime and genius, crime and the human condition."

"Sounds heavy," said Ganning dismissively. He didn't like to hear this sort of university language. Maybe he should give Howard this bloke's card.

"What happens is," Adrian continued, "that a student, a poor, feckless student, murders a moneylender, with an axe, to save his sister from a loveless marriage. His name is Raskolnikov."

"A student called Rascalwhatever kills a moneylender with an axe."

"Yes, but this woman, this capitalist pig, is worthless. She's evil. She has nothing to give. She's a leech. She feeds off the poor and treats her simple sister like a chattel. Raskolnikov decides to kill and rob her to use the money for good deeds, that's what he intends, and he does it, gets away with it. It's the perfect crime."

Doesn't sound like old Agatha Christie, thought Ganning. That was the sort of crime writing he enjoyed. Six posh people in a country house getting slowly poisoned by the butler's cat's ear wax.

"So what happens?"

"This is only the beginning."

"What? He gets a taste for it and does a Hannibal Lecter?"

"No," said Adrian, slightly exasperated, but he'd had this conversation with a hundred different strangers from Amsterdam to Karkov and could recite it in his sleep in three languages. "Once Raskolnikov kills the money lender and gets away with it, it opens a huge new vista of sensations for him. He begins to feel like a human being. He experiences guilt, sorrow, morality, spiritualism. Of course, the guilt is the punishment and it starts even before he'd killed the old woman. And the guilt leads to his confession and imprisonment, the love of his life, but also his redemption. Don't you see? Through murder Raskolnikov becomes a man."

Ganning nodded and passed Adrian another cigarette. This bloke was talking bollocks. He didn't give a shit about some Russian book. Russians were crap. You couldn't sell them anything unless it was a cabbage cookery course.

"So what's the big deal," he said.

"Don't you understand?"

"Yeah, I do," said Ganning, lying. "But I don't know why you're in such a stew about it. I'm a man and I've not killed anyone."

"But, Mr. Ganning, don't you see? I am Raskolnikov."

"So you're a bloke out of a book?"

"No, but I wanted to be. You see, when I first read the book, well, it struck a million cords. Reading the book made me feel like I was some antique harp abandoned in an attic for centuries and then some beautiful creature came along and played the most stirring music. I'd dropped out of university because I had no money and debts and stuff and I ended up on the dole in some south London bedsit. There was nothing to do. Nobody would give me a job and I was at such a loose end, full of schemes about how to get on, but I had no way of doing anything and then I read the book and it all made sense. I had to do something, something to feel."

Ganning had never heard anything so pathetic in his life. It was a great advert for workfare as far as he was concerned. And there were always jobs for people who wanted to sell. The dirtbag violently scratched his head, as if his hair was alive with lice. Ganning ordered another round.

"So you needed to feel. What did you do?"

"I sought out a moneylender."

"What you killed someone?" Ganning's voice hit a shocked crescendo of pitch. This bloke was a nutter. He should march him down the Gestapo station right now.

"No, no," said Adrian, shaking his head in a way that made Ganning feel stupid for missing something unsaid. "I travelled. Across Europe. Hitching and begging. I experienced great deprivation, hunger, exposure and illness. I made it to St. Petersburg just as it was renamed, when it became Dostoyevsky's city again, and there I began my quest for a person so redundant I could bludgeon their brains out and become a man." Adrian forced an angelic pose, palms together across the lapels of his coat, rising up on his toes. "But no candidate appeared. As soon as I got to know my prey I began to understand them and so forgive them. I made the acquaintance of gangsters and pushers, bankers and fascists, but there was no one that fitted the bill. I scoured all of Russia and eastern Europe. Even in Serbia I was disappointed. Then I thought I should do it at random. Anyone would do. The poetry is in the action not the motive. I realised I should learn from Raskolnikov."

"Learn from the rascal."

"Yes. That it is futile. It would never work. All I would get is guilt. And in this realisation I concluded that I'd already suffered enough. The suffering was in the quest. I decided to go home."

"Thank God for that," said Ganning. He was rather bored by the conversation and his cock was getting itchier and itchier. "Look mate. I've got to scoot."

"I didn't think a cretin like you would understand," Adrian laughed, raising his head to the ceiling. He howled until his skin flushed a sunset pink and his eyes began to water. The whole bar turned and stared at Ganning as if he'd done something wrong, that he, Steve Ganning, was picking up a rentboy or buying drugs. Adrian thumped his oily fist on the bar three times.

"Fuck you," Ganning sneered, and trounced out of the bar. Adrian wrapped his coat around himself in a theatrical flourish and swept out after him.

"Wait, wait," he called, as he hopped up the steps. The Fat Man didn't stop, pretending he'd not heard, hurrying his stride, stomping across the glittering pavements. Adrian ran a little and, catching up, grabbed his shoulder. "Can't you smell it?" he exclaimed.

"What?"

"In the air. The stench. The fumes of money. Poison in the air. A miasma of currency. Man gets used to everything, the beast. But replanning, fatso, that's what Raskolnikov dreams of, as he makes for the moneylender's flat, replanning, rebuilding the city for the people."

The dirtbag was flapping his arms about, pointing at the sky with red neon crescents floating over his face.

Ganning was right. This bloke was nuts. He stood to his full height and put his hand into his jacket.

"Here," he said. "Take this and fuck off." He rolled a hundred marks into his cigarette packet and forced it into Adrian's hand. "Buy yourself something to eat or get a bed for the night."

"I don't want your money," Adrian laughed.

"Take it," said Ganning, flagging down a cab. As it pulled up, the dirtbag tried to thrust the packet into Ganning's coat. "Ungrateful wanker," Ganning spat, climbing in. "Romerburg Hotel," he said to the driver as they pulled off, leaving the dirt-bag arsing about in the road.

"We have such a problem with the refugees," said the driver. "We should send them all back to the Yugoslavia."

"That ain't a refugee," Ganning replied. "It's one of our lot."

Adrian leapt into the centre of the street as the tail lights of Ganning's ride disappeared behind him. The bonnet of another taxi stopped only inches short of his legs. Scrambling in, he ordered the driver to follow the cab and tapped the hatchet he'd stolen in Minsk, strung in a sling sewn into his great coat, think-ing: "after all this time I have found you."

Ganning couldn't face another beer cellar. He was tired and the dirtbag had left an unpleasant taste in his mouth. Even Howard wasn't that bad. Supping a quick brandy in the Romerburg's bar, he decided to get an early night. He'd drawn a blank on the first night and remembered how much he'd looked forward to the lonely excitement of urgent hotel room sex. Even so, he had four more evenings in Frankfurt. It was just like miss-ing the first kick of a penalty shoot-out. The game wasn't over yet. The upholstery creaked as he got up, brushing past foyer palms, admiring the cut of his suit in the gallery of mirrors and chrome.

There was a different girl on reception, young, pretty, hair tied up into a chignon. Ganning immediately wanted to untie and unfold it around her bare shoulders as she clambered undressed on top of him.

"Hi," he said, holding out a hand for a shake. "Steve Ganning. Room sixty-five." The girl smiled and coyly shook his paw. "Nice hotel," he said. "I'm impressed."

"I'm glad you're enjoying your stay," she said, in impeccable English.

"Nice town Frankfurt. You from here?"

"Oh no. A small village in Bavaria. But Frankfurt, it's OK. A bit big for me. I like more room."

"Yeah, I know what you mean. Come from a small town myself. I miss it too. The countryside and all that." This was a lie. Ganning had lived in London all his life and rarely left it. But it was important to establish common ground with a client. "Hey. What time do you knock off?"

"Knock off?" she said, bemused.

"Finish work."

"Twenty-three hundred. Half an hour."

"Why don't you come and have a drink with me?" said Ganning, flashing his eyes, "we can compare country stories, when you knock off."

"Maybe," she said, but her delivery gave away no hint of enthusiasm. Ganning realised he sounded desperate and she probably heard this request four or five times day.

"What's your name?"

"Maria."

"Well Maria, room sixty-five. I'm sure you know where it is, if you fancy a drink."

"Maybe." She frowned.

Ganning took his key and felt his confidence take another dip. He summoned the lift and by the time he'd reached his room he'd forgotten about her. Turning on CNN, he loosened his Liberty tie and rummaged in airport carrier bags for the bottle of whisky he'd bought at Heathrow. Half-filling a tumbler, he sat on the end of the double bed, watching television pictures of a new Bosnian army offensive and some militia atrocity in the States. The world was full of nutters, he thought. Grainy footage of a Russian assault on a Chechen stronghold drifted across the screen, soldiers in streets, sludge grey and porridge white, tracer fire over rooftops and tower blocks. Ganning stared about the room, studying the plush velvet curtains, that nice soft yellow colour, and the chandelier and the trestle tables, the bed sagging under his weight.

He stayed there, waiting for the business news, until his bladder began to tighten and beg him to empty it. He left his tumbler on top of the TV and undid his flies as he made for the bathroom. It was out in his hand as he heard the knock on the door. Cock in one hand, he punched the air with his other. Every salesman makes his own luck. Luck follows the players.

He shouted "come in" from the bathroom and heard the door open. Pissing stridently, he watched the arc splash and bubble in the bowl. He'd read somewhere that a man's arc of piss gives him the early instinct to build, to exchange, to sell. He washed his hands and slicked back the sides of his hair, posing and grinning in the steel-framed mirror, thinking that Maria may already be taking off her clothes, slipping out of that alluring uniform, shimmying out of a skirt, its waistband sliding down around stocking tops and suspenders, her hand unbuttoning the blouse, revealing the milky globes harnessed by a wonderbra, the bow tie loose around her neck. Ganning pushed the door open, edging around the corner and into the room.

"Hello," he said. "Glad you could make it."

Then he stopped, dumb-struck. Howard was standing in the middle of the room, in gloves and coat, briefcase in hand.

"Sorry. I know it's late," Howard said, sheepishly.

"What the fuck are you doing here?" shouted Ganning, the sinking slide of his jowls reversed by a detonation of pique.

"Steve, I thought we could talk."

"Eight o'clock. On the stand. Now fuck off." What was this little shit doing at this time of night? Howard hunched into his shoulders.

"But I want to talk to you Steve. I just feel that you're always being so hard on me. I just wanted your advice. I thought you could give me some...tips." There was a cringing, whinging in

Howard's voice. Ganning could see the case twitch at his side, ruffling the flanks of his damp coat. Weakness. Absence of composure. Lack of confidence. Inability to inspire belief. Ganning had had enough of these people.

"OK," he said, realising he couldn't put this off any longer and not bothered anymore about the repercussions within his team. "I was going to wait until we got back to the office Howard, but there's no easy way to say this. You're fired."

"But why?" Howard snapped, his forehead crinkling, flushing.

"You're a crap salesman. I only want go-getters in my team."

"But I sold three books today. Forty-five thousand pounds."

"I don't care. Get Miriam to book you a flight for tomorrow."

"But Steve, I haven't done anything wrong."

"No arguments. I've made an executive decision."

Ganning revelled in his hardness. Every textbook, every course he'd been on, would back him up. Howard didn't fit the company identity and therefore had no identity. Ganning was doing the best thing for the company.

Howard wiped a hand across his fringe.

"I can't believe you're doing this to me."

"Get out," barked Ganning.

"Can't we talk this through?"

"Get out or I'll have you thrown out."

"But...."

Ganning turned and stomped along the bed, pulling the phone violently off its handset. He dialled zero for reception and waited for an answer. Behind him Howard began to unravel. What had he done to deserve this? He was doing well. He was doing his job. He'd only been married six months and his wife was already pregnant. The world went yellow in his eyes, incomprehension, compression. He flicked the catches of the briefcase. Ganning stuttered "come on, come on", into the receiver. The hatchet fell out onto the bedspread, a half-roll, the chandelier light glinting off the edge.

Howard had paced about in his hotel room all night, going over and over his problems with Steve, paranoid he was about to be fired. He knew it was personal. Whatever he did Steve picked him apart. He ridiculed him in front of the other executives, he never said a friendly word; he only ever barracked and shouted, spoke without looking into his eyes, making Howard feel like some insect or carrion bird.

When he decided to come over and see Steve he took the emergency fire hatchet as a symbol. He was going to bury the hatchet, man to man. He thought Steve would admire balls and courage. He thought they'd share a drink and Howard could get it out and say : "Yes, we've buried the hatchet." Steve liked props, flip charts, overheads, acetate diagrams. Imaginative application of props enhanced a selling technique. Howard felt the wood slide along his palm.

Ganning dropped the phone. Howard had quivered and paused, brandishing the shaft high before everything blurred. The first blow, with the back of the hatchet, probably only stunned Ganning, but then, once this shell of restraint shattered, once he'd snapped the line into the unknown, Howard couldn't stop. Blow after blow, Ganning's face became an orange pulp, his nose became a pin cushion of bone fragments. Howard couldn't stop until Ganning stopped struggling. His face was a red basketball with a gaping puncture for a mouth.

Then Howard was up against the wall, gibbering, yelping. Murder, murder, he'd committed murder. Everything in the room changed in his vision, morphed into octagonal planes, nothing possessed curves, the world honeycombed. Howard sobbed, Ganning was dead; Howard was stamped against the wall as the television blinked shifting projections across Ganning's plump, red-running shape. Panting, Howard thought he might lose control of his breathing but time settled him. Time crawled. He was outside of time, transfixed, alone. He slid down the wall and curled his arms about his head, clamping his eyes shut.

I am Rodion Romanovich Raskolnikov, Adrian thought, as he

padded from the lift towards room sixty-five. It hadn't been easy. There had been security guards and hotel staff to dodge, a conspicuous figure to conceal, conversations to eavesdrop. But Adrian had scoured Europe to find The Fat Man. He'd sought him out in the cafes of Petersburg and the factories of Magnitogorsk, in Transcaucasian hamlets and the Baltic capitals. And after all that he'd found him at the core of the West. The Fat Man wasn't going to get away from him that easily.

Once he'd reached the Romerburg, Adrian had seen The Fat Man sit in the bar, sit and ponder, smoke and drink. He watched him from behind a pillar. When the receptionist was distracted by a check-in, he'd slipped around the side of an ornamental fountain and hid himself in a vine-covered corner. When The Fat Man retrieved his keys, Adrian was listening, listening to his chat up lines and the lecherous twang in his voice. Room sixty-five.

He hadn't meant to give The Fat Man so much time but he'd been holed up, shaking with fear, in the cranny, for three quarters of an hour. But Adrian understood this, understood from Raskolnikov, understood that however hard you tried, murder, even metaphysical murder, would never be a sedate affair. He welcomed the fear, the guilt. It was part of the process. The process was working. He felt a different person as he reached the door. He was about to become human. As he lightly tested the lock, it slid around in his palm. It was open. If The Fat Man was asleep, he wouldn't know what hit him and then Adrian could catch that night-train to Amsterdam before the maid discovered the body. He would have a ten hour head start on the police and unlike Raskolnikov, he wasn't local. He could be eating an English breakfast in Dover before the screaming started. He pushed the door and went in. The light was on and the television babbled.

It was the voice that brought Howard out of the stupor. When he opened his eyes he could still see Steve's bloated body, the silk pillow rosy-stained, the blood on the carpet. But there was someone else in the room, hissing, a muffled, angry voice.

"No, no," it said. "How could this be? All this time I have

searched and then to be caught out like this, to be beaten."
There was a dishevelled black-clad man flapping around the
body, weeping. Howard struggled up.

"Who are you?" he stuttered.

"I am Rodion Romanovich Raskolnikov and you have robbed
me of the perfect crime."

Howard was convinced he was mad or dreaming. This had to
be a nightmare. He was stuck in a hotel room with the battered
corpse of his boss and a nineteenth century Russian anti-hero.

"How could you do this?" wept Raskolnikov. "What was he to
you?"

"It was an accident," sobbed Howard.

"But I will still have it," the black figure croaked. "Fresh
opportunities for redemption." He began to get bigger and bigger in Howard's sight. Taller, thinner, harder, denser. His shadow
loomed like Nosfuratu in some silent horror flick. He put his
hand inside his coat. "I will have it."

It was messier the second time. Howard lashed out with the
hatchet when Raskolnikov produced his own but this time the
edge struck under the jawbone and he felt the impact in his
elbow as the metal met the vertebrae and released a crimson
umbrella of spray. Raskolnikov fell on the bed, twisting and
retching, his hands over his neck, blood jetting through his fingers like a forked hose pipe. He let out a soul-stripping, night-
devouring, white steel scream, for a second, then stopped.

Howard felt nothing. This wasn't real. Soon he'd wake up and
go to the stand and Steve would be swearing at him and ignoring
him all day and Raskolnikov would be back between the covers
of the book in his suitcase where he belonged. Howard was sure
you weren't supposed to like Raskolnikov.

But it was real. The blood pooled on the carpet was real. The
blood on the bedspread was real. The blood up the walls was
real. Howard sat down and studied the two bodies, feeling his
metabolism, his very physiology, alter in the glare of their rolled,
blank eyes.

Then it struck him, what Raskolnikov had said. The perfect crime. Two men found, hatchets in their hands, in a hotel room. They killed each other for reasons unknown. Nobody knew Howard was here. His own hotel was an unmanned guesthouse. He had his own key. Nobody saw him leave. He was wearing gloves. He left no finger prints. He had no blood stains. Nobody had seen him come into the Romerburg either. He walked in after a ten strong party of Americans had hit the desk. It was chaos. And what had he done? Steve was going to ruin his life, take away his ability to feed himself, his wife and baby. And the other man was a lunatic. He'd wanted to kill Steve anyway. He wasn't innocent. Howard knew from his reading that Raskolnikov murdered two innocent people, the moneylender and her sister. Howard had only murdered the guilty and the deranged. If Steve was dead, he could get on with his life. Miriam would be promoted. There would be a vacancy. He smiled to himself, feeling a cold hood of resolution slide over him.

He took the hatchet and slipped into the bathroom, sloshing water on his face to cool down. All he had to do was put the axe in Steve's dead fist, that's all. He grinned a spiky film-poster grin in the mirror.

Then there was a petrified sobbing. He dashed into the bedroom, hatchet in hand. Maria was standing, shaking, gibbering at the end of the bed, her fingers crammed into her mouth, quaking with mortal fear. Howard raised the blade to the level of her head. My God, he thought, I am Raskolnikov after all.

If You Go Down to the Woods Today....

by
David C Wareham

David C Wareham

David has been writing for thirty years. He is probably best known for his work as an herpetologist and has written widely on reptiles and their conservation for both the popular and scientific press. In 1993 his REPTILE AND AMPHIBIAN KEEPER'S DICTIONARY: AN A-Z OF HERPETOLOGY *was published which has since become the standard source of reference.*

He is also a qualified artist and an accomplished photographer, often using his work to illustrate his own articles and that of other authors. This is David's third short fictional story to be published and he is currently working on his first novel.

If You Go Down to the Woods Today....

by

David C Wareham

R on loved the creatures of the wood, and they loved him....
but in a way that he could never have begun to imagine.

It was mid-day and the shade of the woodland's trees provided
welcome relief from the blistering July heat. Ron was sitting
against a tall pine examining a shoe he had just uncovered in the
undergrowth. It was a gent's brogue, size 10, and apart from
some feathery fronds of moss protruding from three of the ornamental perforations, it looked almost new. Who on earth, he
wondered, would venture all this way into the wood and then go
home wearing only one shoe ?

The heel and sole showed hardly any wear at all and the shine
on the black leather was only slightly dulled by dampness. The
lace was still tied in a neat bow. He could understand, perhaps,
someone abandoning an old car in the middle of nowhere, but a
shoe ? And one in such reasonable condition too ? With the lace
still tied ?

He closed his eyes and smiled as he conjured up an image of a
man strolling through the woods, seemingly blissfully unaware
he was missing a shoe, his unshod foot bristling with pine needles and burrs.

Not many used the wood now. At one time it had been the
haunt of laughing children by day and lovers by night but had
long since slipped into neglect. Large areas of stagnant bog now
covered what had once been shady pathways and, in places, the

nettles and briars had become virtually impenetrable.

After a nagging and prolonged back problem had forced him into retiring prematurely Ron had developed an interest in nature and visited the wood as often as possible, each time exploring a little further into its depths in the hope of finding a rare flower or an unusual beetle. He had no family and few friends but had no need for either really. The animals were his friends and he would always bring tasty tit-bits for them. They, in turn, repaid him by filling his visits with beauty and wonder.

A sudden commotion in some nearby bracken distracted Ron's attention. Turning slowly he rolled onto his stomach and peered cautiously around the bole of the tree. He could see the ferns waving, yet there was no wind. He could hear a faint pattering, yet there was no rain. Then it stopped. No movement, no sound.

Ron put the shoe down and was getting up when he saw it. Less than four metres away, and directly in front of him, a rabbit had stumbled from the undergrowth. It was shaking visibly and was obviously aware of some presently unseen danger.

He pressed himself closer to the ground. Movements in the bracken told him something else was present. He held his breath and watched.

Without warning the rabbit opened its mouth, as if gasping for air, and its body shook violently. With a gurgled squeal it raised itself on its haunches and toppled over sideways into the grass. Ron stood up and approached slowly, half expecting the rabbit to bolt into the undergrowth but it didn't move.

Reaching down to pick it up he immediately recoiled. Clinging to its throat, its head buried deep in the rabbit's fur, was an animal Ron had never seen before. The size of a rat, its skin was green, wrinkled and completely hairless. He could see no tail but its hindquarters were partly concealed by the rabbit's body.

Trembling with excitement Ron looked for something with which to prise the little creature from the rabbit. He spotted a withered branch on a nearby tree and ran over to snap it off. It didn't come away easily and it took several seconds of tugging and twisting before it finally broke away.

He could hear a curious crunching sound and turning around his eyes fell upon a staggering spectacle. The rabbit had completely disappeared beneath a mass of writhing green bodies. Oblivious to Ron's presence, they were voraciously gorging themselves on the animal's warm flesh.

Prodding the severed branch into the heaving swarm he tried to dislodge one in order to examine it more closely. At once the creatures scattered, stopping a short distance away to turn and face their unwelcomed intruder. To his astonishment he saw that they ran upright, on their hind legs. This, together with their lack of a tail and typical pointed snouts of most rodents puzzled him.

He stared at them and felt his stomach turn. They were the ugliest, most disgusting animals he had ever seen. He was no expert naturalist but was used to most animals. He had handled many kinds, from spiders and bats to snakes and toads, without any fear or foreboding but these unsettled him and made the blood chill in his veins.

Instead of taking flight, as most other animals do when threatened or disturbed, these stood their ground in apparent defiance.

Ron lifted the branch and swept it down in an arc over their heads. They hissed loudly like angry serpents causing him to jump back.

Again he brought down the branch. Lower this time, striking one of them, more accidentally than deliberate, on the side of its head. It let out a high-pitched scream and fell stunned to the ground. The others, now aroused and undaunted by Ron's sudden onslaught, began inching towards him.

Ron took a few steps back and felt something at his feet. Looking down he saw the carcass of the rabbit. It had been ripped apart and its steaming entrails partly devoured. White fragments of chewed bone protruded from the reddened fur and the eyeless skull had been cracked open like an egg. He placed the branch beneath the rabbit's body and tossed it towards the creatures. It landed heavily on a dozen or so and the air was immediately filled with their shrill screams.

Suddenly he was aware of something on his leg. He swiped his hand instinctively against his calf, knocking the creature onto his boot. It sat there for a moment looking up at him with black, soulless eyes and hissing through clenched yellow teeth. Ron kicked out his leg and hurled the creature high into the air. It crashed into the gnarled trunk of an old oak and fell limply into the briars beneath.

At first he had estimated thirty or so but their number had swelled to at least twice that. He was getting worried. Indeed, he was getting frightened. He began to shout and sweep his branch back and forth across the ground, bowling the creatures over like skittles. But still they came at him.

Somehow, two had managed to grab the branch as it swept over them and were now crawling along its length towards Ron's hand. He spotted them and yelled out in alarm. He tried to shake them off but couldn't. He dared not release the branch for, at that moment, it was his only weapon.

Another was starting to climb his boot. Using the thick lace as an easy foothold, it scrambled upward beneath his corduroys. On reaching the top of his sock it opened its mouth wide and sank its jagged teeth into tensed muscle. Ron shouted with the pain and the branch dropped from his grasp. One of the creatures fell with it but the other, having succeeded in reaching Ron's hand, hung on to his thumb with its teeth.

In a frenzy of agonised terror, Ron beat his hands rapidly over his shaking body. As he slapped his legs he made contact with two bodies and they slipped shrieking from beneath his trousers. He bent over and slammed his fist into the earth crushing the one that was clinging to it. As it lay squirming in the earth he could see it still had a mouthful of his skin between its teeth.

Free of them for the moment he stood up and looked around, shuddering at what he saw. He was surrounded by them. There were dozens and dozens of them, perhaps a hundred or more, all standing perfectly still, watching Ron and waiting intently for his next move.

He could not see the branch he had dropped and wondered what to do next. He thought about climbing a tree but what if they could climb too ? No, although the trees seemed to be offering sanctuary in their leafy canopies, climbing one seemed too much of a risk at that moment. Such an escape route could prove to be a dead-end and there was no way he was going to spend the night in a Scots pine in the middle of the woods, in the dark, with those green mini-monsters from Hell waiting at the bottom for him to fall out.

Ron's shirt was dark and heavy with sweat in the cloying heat and humidity of the afternoon and it felt as if it was glued to his skin like a soggy sticking plaster. He had to think fast for the creatures were almost upon him. He decided there was only one thing to do. Ripping off his shirt, he rolled it up and threw it into their midst. It was visible for just a second and then it was gone, swamped and devoured beneath a mass of writhing green bodies excited by the smell of Ron's body, his sweat, his fear. Whilst they were thus distracted he drew a deep breath and leapt into the air.

Yelling at the top of his voice, he set off running. The creatures, taken by surprise by this sudden and unexpected action, scattered in all directions. Most of them dived safely into the thick undergrowth but a few rushed straight into Ron's path where they were crushed beneath his boots.

Several of the more agile ones threw themselves at his legs and feet in a final desperate attempt to get a hold on him. But he moved too fast for them. They were knocked away and sent sprawling, over and over each other, into the foliage.

Smashing his way through the tangled brambles, cursing as the thorns ripped and tore at his already bloodied limbs, he ran blindly from the nightmare. Not wanting to turn around lest he should trip, he prayed that he would soon outdistance them.

As he ran he noticed that the undergrowth was getting thicker and the trees denser. In his panic to escape he had plunged still deeper into the wood and was now well and truly lost. He had not delved this far before but, as long as he had left those things behind him he didn't really care.

It was no good. He had to look back. His legs were about to give up on him, his back was aching and his heart was about to burst. He wouldn't be able to run much further anyway for the undergrowth was becoming much too thick. He stole a glance over his shoulder. To his great relief he couldn't see them. Not a single one. He looked again. Just to make sure. Yes, he had indeed lost them. He half laughed, half cried with joy. He turned back to see the ground suddenly fall away beneath him. Legs and arms flailing, he stepped out into nothingness.

He came to rest abruptly in a small rhododendron and realised he had fallen into a crater-shaped pit some four or five metres deep. Had it not been for the shrub breaking his fall, he would almost certainly have broken something. He leaned against the pit wall and consciously tried to slow his pounding heart and regulate his rapid breathing. He began to feel pain in parts of his body that he hadn't realised he had.

He desperately wanted to drink from the shallow pool that had formed in the bottom of the pit but it was full of tiny, wriggling insects which quickly put him off the idea. Instead he washed the congealing blood from his hands and arms, the cool water soothing his scarlet wounds and refreshing his sweating brow.

A pair of yellow butterflies danced in a shaft of sunlight over the pool and Ron watched them as they disappeared. one after the other, over the lip of the pit. When they had gone there was no movement and no sound. He would be following them in a moment and he smiled as he drank in the stillness with a loud sigh.

The wood was silent now. His yelling and hasty passage through it must have frightened off every living thing he thought, reflecting for a moment upon his horrific encounter of just a short while ago. In retrospect it all seemed too fantastic, too incredible. That sort of thing just doesn't happen in an English woodland. He would have to tell someone when he got home. He would have to report it. . . to find out what those animals. . . things. . . were.

Ron could hear the distant rumble of traffic on the motorway and, for the first time, considered what a friendly sound it was. He would use it as a guide to help find his way home but would have to move quickly now. His watch was broken but he guessed it was early evening for the light was fading fast.

He eased his tired, aching body up the pit wall. The sides were of clay and he lost his footing several times. Finally, he managed to grasp a root protruding through the top of the pit's rim and, with a grunt, hauled himself up.

Ron peered over the edge and gasped in dismay. The entire

woodland floor was a mass of small, green, wrinkled figures advancing slowly and deliberately towards the pit, their yellow, festering teeth gnashing at the thought of the feast to come.

He slid back down into the belly of the pit, sobbing uncontrollably and watched helplessly as they clambered in after him.

At first he attempted to swat them away as they swarmed over his body tearing at his flesh but there was so many of them it was pointless to resist. He opened his mouth and screamed but it was swiftly stifled as he sank deeper beneath the heaving mass.

Mercifully, he did not take long to die. In a matter of seconds they were inside him, chewing at his heart and nibbling at his very soul. That which they could not eat immediately was ripped out and carried away to the hollow trees from whence they had come, to be savoured at a later time.

When dawn broke the next morning there was nothing to say Ron had ever been there. Nothing except a reddish-brown stain on the floor of the pit. . . . and a single boot, its lace still tied.

Ron had always enjoyed feeding the wild creatures of the wood, and they were always grateful for his visits. This visit in particular would sustain them for some time. . . or at least. . . until someone else happened by.

Shopping for Katie

Nathan's Friend

Two short stories

by

Mark Cantrell

Mark Cantrell

Mark writes to live and lives to write, but since writing for him is an endless process of smoking cigarettes he might have a problem here. By day he is a journalist, covering the exciting cut and thrust of the global textile business. By night he wrestles with the muse, not to mention the endless distractions offered by a PC, and strives to make sense of a churning imagination. It must work: he has written numerous short stories (some of which have been published) and hundreds of articles. He has also written two novels.

Shopping for Katie

by

Mark Cantrell

Katie was such a wonderful child. A dream come true for Lynn and myself. I suppose all parents say that, but we had been trying for years to have children. Never with any success. Imagine our despair when we both discovered we were sterile. That our dream was shattered, that we would never become a real family.

Lynn took this hard. She wasn't a real woman unless she could have a child of her own - so she kept saying. I had to keep my own emotions hidden, yet inside I was as upset as she was. I needed to be strong to help her you see. To give her some kind of support. Yet it never seemed to be enough; the sound of her weeping would often fill the house.

These scenes always followed a visit to friends. The photographs would come out, Lynn would play with the children and be all smiles. It was like watching a different woman then. She came alive, her eyes were bright and she laughed a lot. Then at home she released her tears. I was watching her fall apart and there was nothing I could do.

Several times I tried to talk to her about adoption, but Lynn wouldn't have anything to do with it. Our child would be of our own flesh and blood, or we would have none at all. That's how our marriage continued and it was becoming unbearable, I can tell you.

There were some - rare - moments of pleasure. We shared in the joy of our friends as their children grew older. But it was always second hand, never our own. Then I heard about Wonder Child and our lives were turned around.

Wonder Child was a company specialising in treating childless couples. And they were no fly by nights - here today, gone tomorrow. They had been around for years and, by all accounts, they had a solid reputation. I wouldn't have bothered with them myself. I suppose it's because I'm a bio-engineering technician, so I've seen enough of the industry's fuck-ups to be somewhat wary. Lynn was so eager, however, that I couldn't possibly ignore the chance.

And so we finally had our first child.

I can still remember when little Katie was born. Lynn was over-joyed. So was I for that matter. I was a father at last. After all those years of disappointment we had a real family. Naturally, we became walking clichés.

The birth itself was nothing. So I'm told. Lynn's labour was easy enough compared to some, though not painless as many are. My wife insisted on going through the pain of natural childbirth. It assists maternal bonding or some such thing. (What can I say? Lynn reads a lot of women's magazines.) So there she lay, crying out with each contraction, covered in sweat while I held her hand and offered encouragement. It really was miraculous how our first child came into being: a miracle of technology.

What was it Dave, our client advisor had said? Ah yes - the most natural birth modern technology can provide. Well it certainly was impressive. I saw the pleasure on Lynn's face as they removed the virtuality headset and the techs brought in little Katie, still wet and bloody from the birthing vats. I remember grinning like an idiot as they placed my daughter in Lynn's arms. She was perfect, right down to her little pink toes.

"Congratulations!" Dave said, slapping me on the back. "You have a beautiful daughter."

After that we went outside, leaving Lynn and the baby to rest and become acquainted. I puffed happily on my complimentary cigar even though I didn't smoke. We discussed the company's After Birth Service plan but my mind wasn't really on it. My eyes kept straying to the doors and my new family on the other side. Two hours later both Lynn and the baby were home.

You should have seen Lynn's face. She glowed with happiness when she placed Katie in the cot I had built from a kit. During the nine months that Katie was growing in the birthing vat I had converted the back bedroom into a nursery. Lynn had bought all the furnishings and toys and all the other paraphernalia a newborn child needs. I had not seen her so happy since we were first married.

Well, that was the birth of my child, my little girl. But it wasn't when she was born, not to me. No. For me that took place ten months before. The actual birth was just a matter of the biological mechanics that have taken place for time immemorial, albeit with a few man-made modifications.

Katie was born in our hearts and minds during that first meeting with Dave. All the red tape had been sorted out a week before. We had signed the contract and cell samples were taken from both of us. This session was... well, I suppose there's no other way of saying it, to design our daughter.

You can't know what it's like unless you've been through it. It's something you never forget. I remember it so clearly, more than the birth itself. Lynn and I had been so nervous when we walked into Reception at the Wonder Child branch in the high street. There were other hopefuls there, like us eager to have that perfect child.

Looking back, I can't see why we should have been so nervous. The staff was so friendly and went out of their way to make us feel at ease. I guess it's something to do with the baby-making business that fills everyone involved with a warm glow.

Coffee was made available while we waited for our advisor. I studied the place as my wife flicked through the brochures scattered in strategic places. I could sense Lynn's nerves as she studied the happy couples helped by Wonder Child. Boys and girls stared back at my wife from scenes of family contentment and gratitude. In ten months we would be one of those happy families. I confess I couldn't wait.

A smart young man in a suit walked over and greeted us pleasantly: our client advisor. "Mr and Mrs Richards," he said, shaking me firmly by the hand. "It's a pleasure to meet you. My name's David Turner but I'd be happy if you called me Dave. I'll be your guide into parenthood over the next ten months."

The man led us to a booth at the back of the reception area. It was a cosy set up. If you're familiar with most offices then you'll know how most of the time there's a barrier between you and the corporate face. They call it a desk. That wasn't the case here. We sat on a little couch. Dave sat next to us, turning so that he could face Lynn and I.

Dave pulled out a notebook computer and flipped up the lid. As it popped open a remote screen came to life on the wall. The company's logo was displayed - a baby's smiling face - on an ever-changing background of alpha-helical molecules that I knew instantly as DNA.

The display changed when Dave hit a key. Up came our credit details, personal history and contract. "Ah, I see you're hoping for a daughter," Dave said brightly, a mere formality since the gene programmers would be making our hope a certainty.

"Well, if I can take the rest of your details...."

"There won't be any problems will there?" My wife asked. "I mean, she will be our daughter won't she?"

Dave smiled at my wife and placed a comforting hand on her arm. "Don't worry Mrs Richards," he said solemnly, "your daughter will be your own flesh and blood as much as if you carried her yourself. Our programmers work from your own cell material and the child is grown in the most natural environment possible.

"In fact, you made the best decision in coming to us. Our rivals are still using metal and glass vats, not very healthy for the baby in my view. We use the latest state of the art birthing technology - a process pioneered here at Wonder Child. Your baby will be grown in specially bred wombs. The only conventional technology will be the feeder unit that supplies oxygen and nutrients to the womb. Only the best is provided here Mrs Richards. It's the most natural birth modern technology can provide."

That satisfied Lynn and Dave proceeded to take down Katie's details. The image of a child appeared as he typed in our preferences and slowly the image began to grow....

"Attributes?" Dave asked.

"Intelligence... only not too intelligent. We don't want to put men off when she's older. She should be kind, considerate... a sense of humour."

Dave laughed, not unkindly. "We can do something as regards

intelligence, Mrs Richards, but the rest... well, that's down to pro-gramming inputs we can't provide here at Wonder Child. Now what about any particular talents?"

"Oh! I'm not sure. I hadn't really thought. Music perhaps? I've always thought it would be nice to have a musician in the family. Or sport, maybe. What do you think John?"

My wife's question broke my quiet contemplation. I was fasci-nated by the image on the screen. It showed a five year old girl. My daughter was growing before my eyes, the future possibilities unfolding. Unclear, until we finally filled in all the gaps.

"I don't know, why not both?" I replied. And that was that. My daughter was to be a sporty musician.

"Now how about physical attributes?"

"She must be beautiful," my wife instantly replied.

"Mrs Richards, looking at the pair of you I know your daughter will be just that without our programmers touching a thing!"

I smiled at the sincere piece of salesmanship. Still, my daughter was beautiful so I suppose he wasn't lying.

"By the physical attributes I mean certain cosmetic alterations. One of the wonders we can perform here is to make slight but very startling modifications to your child so that she'll be the best com-plement for the both of you."

"I hadn't really thought about it. I suppose she'll be pretty much similar to us, John?"

I just grunted in a noncommittal fashion. Shopping decisions were Lynn's affair as far as I was concerned. Dave wasn't put off by our indecision though.

"If you would allow me, Mrs Richards," he said suavely, "might I suggest an aryan style would suit you down to the ground? Blonde hair and blue eyes are very fashionable at the moment. And as you know, gentlemen prefer blondes."

That was a nice touch. I suppose every parent worries about their offspring meeting the right person in years to come. As much as they worry about the quality of the people they do become involved with. It's one of those things I suppose. In any case my wife liked the idea. Mind you, once I'd seen the result so did I.

At the end of the session there she was simulated before me on that computer screen. And she stirred most unfatherly thoughts I have to say. Katie was an angel, and I thought of the hearts she would be breaking in years to come. She had already broken mine. Katie was the perfect child. All we could have hoped for.

That was how my little Katie was really born. As you already know, we took her home ten months later and we settled down into domestic, family bliss.... Almost.

Don't get me wrong. As the years passed, Katie proved every bit the beautiful child we had seen displayed on that screen. There were all the milestones in a child's development that parents have gone gooey over for generations; that first word, toddling, walking, nursery. On the other hand you've got the down side; dirty nappies, teething, crying at all hours, potty training, childish tantrums. Still, you take the good with the bad, don't you?

Those first years were pretty trying. Lynn and I were used to being a couple. Now we were a threesome. A baby takes some looking after; we weren't quite prepared for the grim realities of parenthood. Sometimes I wished we'd never had a child. But when I looked at Lynn playing with Katie, such thoughts evaporated in to thin air.

Katie grew up like any normal child. She was a good kid, well behaved, happy. Of course she was naughty too, had the odd tantrum. I mean, she was our little angel, but she had a devilish, mischievous side too. What child doesn't? There were moments when my darker side wished we could have programmed obedience into Katie. But who wants a robot for a daughter? I certainly wouldn't. There was nothing about Katie we would have changed. Except for one thing.

When Katie was five she had the most luxuriant blonde hair. Lynn and I were unhappy with it. Somehow it just wasn't us, you know? It's always the way isn't it? You see something in the shop and you think to yourself that's just right. Of course once you get it in the home setting somehow it's not quite right after all. That's the way we felt about Katie's hair. I suppose we allowed ourselves to be guided too much by Dave. Indecision is a salesman's best friend. If the client isn't sure hit them with an option. Chances are they'll take it. We certainly did.

Matters were easily fixed. I bought one of those new

GenChrome hair colourants. How Katie struggled. We had to promise her that pet rabbit she'd been after for months before she would settle down. Even then Lynn had to hold her firm and keep soothing her as I prepared the application. I still can't see what all the fuss was about. I found the vein easily enough and in the blink of an eye the application was in Katie's bloodstream.

After that we were waiting impatiently to see if the application had taken. After a few weeks she had a good few inches of auburn hair. I had to buy Katie a second rabbit to placate her after I cut away the blonde.

"Don't worry, it'll grow back," I told her. Katie still sulked, until I produced the second rabbit. She loved those animals. She would play with them every chance she got. You know, I never had the heart to tell her they were artificial.

Katie's childhood was like any other, just the usual vicissitudes. I don't know if the gene programmers had done anything to upgrade her intelligence. Personally I'm sceptical about such things. In any case, she was a bright girl. She excelled at school, coming top in most of her subjects. Except maths. Katie hated that subject.

As for her musical and sporting talents, there wasn't much evidence of those. Sure she was average at school in any sporting activity. But she never displayed any musical abilities of any particular note. Looking back, I'm hardly surprised. The talent may have been there but Lynn and myself have hardly been musical enthusiasts. So I guess the background was never there for her talents to flourish. I can't say I'm sorry, but we were a little disappointed at the time.

Ah! How could I have felt disappointment at my little girl, my bright, talented little angel? My Katie; not when she was to leave us so suddenly.

I'll remember that day as long as I live. It was a Monday morning, not long after Katie's seventeenth birthday. The weather was bright and cheery, not exactly the herald of bad tidings. Lynn's scream was terrible to hear. I ran out of the bathroom clad only in my pyjama bottoms and my face covered in shaving foam. Lynn was outside Katie's room, crying hysterically.

"What's wrong?" I asked.

Lynn cried out Katie's name in a strangled sob and pulled me into her room. I couldn't believe what I saw. There was my little girl, barely breathing. Her pallor was deathly pale with dark rings around her eyes. My heart leapt into my mouth. Katie had rarely been ill as a child and now she seemed close to death. I couldn't understand what was wrong with her. The night before she had seemed in perfect health.

I don't remember much of what followed. Obviously I called an ambulance because my next clear memory is of the hospital. Lynn had stopped crying as we waited anxiously. I could tell by the way that she sat that her calm was only a brittle, skin-deep facade. She could break down at any moment.

"Katie will be all right," I said and put my arm around Lynn. She buried her face in my chest and clung to me tightly. We sat like that for some time. It was the worst period of my life. I felt so help-less. My little girl was fighting for her life and there wasn't a damn thing I could for her. Except wait.

Dave arrived an hour later. Over the years he had become a friend of the family. That was normal; Wonder Child liked to stress that their clients and staff were like one big happy family. He had been like an uncle to Katie; an uncle to God knows how many children developed at their facilities.

"I heard about Katie," he said. "Is there anything I can do?"

"Nothing. The doctors are with her now. All we can do is wait."

Dave guided me a few steps away from Lynn. She just stared into space as though she didn't know where she was. "How's Lynn?" Dave enquired.

"Not too good," I shrugged. I wasn't feeling so good myself. Dave just nodded and looked away a moment. I could feel his anguish, but I could sense it had to do with more than Katie's ill-ness.

"John.... Christ! I don't know how best to say this."

"Let's sit down."

I walked to the other side of the waiting room. Lynn still appeared cut off from the world at large.

"The doctors sent us tissue samples. It's a standard procedure for any of our children when something like this happens."

"Like what happens?"

"Haven't the doctors told you anything?"

I just shook my head. Anxiety had momentarily taken away my capacity for speech.

"I suppose they've been too busy. The thing is, Katie has suffered... ah... massive control gene failure. I don't know why that should have happened after all this time, but...."

"What the Hell is control gene failure?" I finally managed to say.

Dave looked away when he replied. "Think of it like cancer. It happens very fast and the cells basically forget what they are. It's a mess...."

I couldn't believe what I was hearing so I stood up and walked away. A rage was building up inside me and I wanted to hit something, someone, maybe Dave. Instead I did nothing, just let the emotions build inside me, buried deep. It's something I learned to do in our childless years, a way of coping with life's shit. I turned to face Dave. The sight of his pained, apologetic face somehow stirred some of that anger to rise from the depths.

"Are you telling me you didn't program Katie right?" I shouted, shocking Lynn from her private world. "Is it? Is my daughter dying because you fucked up?"

"John, please... I'm just a company interface. I only know what they tell me...."

"Shut up! You can get back to your bosses and tell them to do something for Katie. They can sort out this mess."

Dave had gone pale. Maybe I was too hard on him, I don't know, but he was their salesman. That made him just as responsible for my daughter's illness as those who programmed her. At least in my eyes.

"I'm sorry, John. That won't be happening."

"Why not?"

"John, please calm down. You're not making this any easier," he almost whispered. I grabbed his collar and dragged him to his feet. Dave couldn't look me in the eyes when he continued. "The company is no longer liable for Katie's genome. You used an unauthorised genetic application on her. That voided the company's liability. I'm sorry."

Those words hit me physically. I was a bio-technician, I should have known better. I should have read the small print. Instead I acted the fool and killed my daughter on the ridiculous whim that she didn't quite match my personal style. I told Dave to go, that I never wanted to see his face again. I couldn't believe what he had just told me. The man had been at Katie's Christening....

Katie was pronounced dead an hour later. I'll say no more than that. The emotional stress was too great and I don't want to relive what I went through with Lynn. The funeral took place a fortnight later. Dave sent an elaborate wreath so maybe there were some sincere feelings in him somewhere. But I haven't seen him since that day in the hospital.

All I can think of now is why me? Why was my daughter taken from me? Out of all the hundreds upon hundreds of children living normal, healthy lives thanks to Wonder Child, why did mine have to go so horribly wrong? Who should I blame? Myself?

Yet it is my fault in a way. I shouldn't have used that application on her. But I know enough to say that it didn't kill her. It only affects functional hair follicles. No. Wonder Child fucked up somewhere when they programmed my little girl. Maybe their debugging simulators weren't quite up to scratch. Whatever, the responsibility was theirs, except for one minor little legal technicality.

Perhaps they could have cured Katie. Perhaps not. Now that Katie is dead it doesn't really matter. Nothing can fill the gaping hole left in my life.

And as for Lynn, well, I have to see her later today. She's apparently making good progress after her breakdown. She still hates me, though. No matter how many times I apologise it falls on deaf ears. I'll apologise again today. I'll say to her: "I'm sorry I voided the warranty on our child."

How many times have I said that now? Maybe today will be different. Maybe today Lynn will forgive me....

©Mark Cantrell

Nathan's Friend

by

Mark Cantrell

TONIGHT was the night Nathan told himself. It was game time: the Mating Game. Despite the annoying lights and the gloom, his eyes scanned the dancing crowd; analysing, searching, hungering for love.

"Where are we?" Richard asked sleepily. "Oh not here again! You'll never pull here. You never do!"

"Shut up," Nathan replied. The alcohol was surging through his body now. Yet it never seemed to blot out Richard's chatter. Perversely it made him worse. Nathan wished he would go away. He could do without the perpetual innuendoes and remorseless jibes. Sometimes he wondered why he bothered with him.

Nathan moved towards the bar where he brazenly studied the women around him. Dare he hope to catch an eye, to converse even? Some of the women noticed his scrutiny and stared back.

"She's looking at you. You're in there!" Fear swept through Nathan. Drink in hand, he fled. Richard laughed at him all the way. "Loser!"

Away from the bar and the dance floor, Nathan occupied a no-man's land; a moment's escape from the pleasures of the flesh. Time to ponder strategy, if only Richard could keep his mouth shut and let the brain do its work.

A girl walked past. She smiled and looked sidelong at Nathan, casting her head down as she brushed nearby. He nearly choked on the surge of panic and quickly walked away. The girl disappeared into the pack.

"You should have grabbed her and stuck your tongue down her

throat!"

"Why don't you piss off?" Nathan said. He took another sip of his beer. Someone jarred his arm, tipping the tepid fluid over him.

"Can't handle the pints, can't handle the bints," Richard sniggered.

"I don't see you doing so well"

"Me? I got nothing to prove. I can have any bint I want. When I want."

Nathan ruefully looked at the dregs of his beer. There was nothing else for it, he would have to get another. Maybe he could lose Richard at the bar? There was always hope.

"Living dangerously aren't we? Your second half!"

"Piss off, this is my third pint."

Nathan fought his way back to the bar. Too many sweating bodies crushed in. Someone stamped on his foot and he was jostled this way and that by the press of bodies.

Everybody was shouting at once, clamouring to be heard over the musical din and each other. The orders came thick and fast, the staff rushing to supply drinks and rake in the cash, sweating into the beer and playing off one customer against another. The barman passed Nathan over again, serving people left, right and behind. Humiliation raised his body temperature, slowly bringing his blood to the boil.

"Mine's a pint," Richard screamed in his ear, sharp pain causing him to miss the barman yet again.

"Get your own!"

"God! You're useless. Let me do it."

Richard stood on the footrest and leaned over. As soon as the barman returned Richard grabbed him and shouted: "A pint of bitter!" The man looked sourly at Richard and shrugged him off, but to Nathan's surprise he poured the pint.

"You grab me again and I'll fucking kill you!" He shouted as Nathan paid.

Richard laughed. "Any time, mate!"

People stared malevolently. The girl who should have been served first mouthed something obscene. The attention was too much. Nathan hurriedly moved away, cursing Richard's brash aggression even as he envied his confidence. It wasn't fair. The

Richards of this world seemed to get everything. While more sensitive souls were brushed aside.

"Not sulking are we?"

"No."

"Good. Drink up. We're gonna play hunt the crumpet!"

An involuntary wince flickered across Nathan's face. Richard was always so crude. He had no respect. Women were just sex on legs, use and discard them, like a surgical syringe, except in this case Richard was the needle.

Some friend. Why did he hang around with Richard? Maybe because no one else would bother with him. And occasionally he could be entertaining.

"Women are people too, you know," he said.

"Oh for God's sake. Do you wanna get laid? Or write poems!"

That cut to the quick. Nathan sipped his beer and turned away to hide his pain. Of course he wanted to get laid. But there had to be more to it than sex. You had to feel something more than lust, he thought, at least a mild liking.

How could Richard go through life like that? Did he never get lonely? Surely, deep inside, he wanted somebody to hang around for longer than a couple of minutes - or half an hour to Richard's internal time frame. Nathan shivered at the cold emptyness of it all. Yet Richard's life seemed more fulfiled than his own. That really rankled.

With a heartfelt sigh of despair he gulped his beer. Would he never find someone? Was he cursed to be forever alone? It was all Richard's fault. He was everything that was obscene about the male of the species. Guilt by association, wasn't that it?

Nathan drained his drink, spilling some of it down his chest. Then he let the glass fall to the floor and moodily kicked it under a seat.

"Finished?" Richard asked disdainfully. "Good. Let's go."

This was it. The moment for which he had been building courage all evening. She stood by herself, leaning against the wall, with a glass held casually in one hand. Nathan's eyes scanned the girl's body. She had an appealing shape, even if the gloom hid most of her features.

Time to act. He walked towards her. The girl didn't move as

Nathan sidled up. He feigned indifference, casually leaned against the wall and glanced around the club. The girl raised her glass and sipped.

"Go on then! Or are you chicken?"

His guts felt rancid from a combination of alcohol and terror. Nerves jittered and it was an effort to control his body. A muscle in his cheek twitched uncontrollably and he prayed it wasn't noticeable.

"Well?"

He couldn't do it. Richard's scorn was rising. Still he couldn't do it. Then his body moved closer to the girl, trembling with fear. She'll tell me to fuck off. They always do. He moved closer. Almost touching. He opened his mouth to speak.

The girl threw the remains of her drink to the floor. The glass bounced off Nathan's hip and poured the dregs down his leg. Richard laughed.

"Oh God! I'm sorry!" The girl cried out.

"That's okay," he replied, "my fault."

The girl walked away, followed by Nathan's rueful gaze. A man appeared from the dance floor and put his arm around her waist.

"Hopeless!"

"She was with someone, didn't you see?"

"So what? You could have had her you useless twat. Prime opportunity. Beer on the balls - what an opening!"

"Why don't you just leave me alone?"

Nathan stomped off into the crowd, disappointed and disgraced. A dull ache throbbed in his chest and his eyes tingled. The world seemed a dim and distant place as he chewed on loneliness.

The music changed, heralding a mass exodus to the bar. Nathan let the tide of bodies carry him along until he was washed up like social jetsam.

Another drink to drown the sorrows. It tasted of water but he didn't care. Richard followed him. Nathan could feel his presence, feel his sneers and his leering assessment of the women that crowded around, women that flaunted themselves to the males in their version of the Game.

A couple embraced amongst the press of bodies, like Siamese twins joined at the lips. Nathan brushed past, averting his gaze but unable to shut them out of his awareness. They seemed so tender, so considerately aware of each other's needs. A pang of jealousy erupted beneath his sternum.

"What a slag! I wonder if he even knows her name?"

"Not everybody's a total shit like you!"

"Oh dear. We are in a bad mood aren't we?"

BACK in no-man's land once more. Not to think this time, instead to brood. The Game was over. He'd had enough. Richard had ruined it, just as he always did.

"Excuse me?"

The sudden intrusion flustered Nathan. He looked up and found himself meeting a woman's gaze. It was the girl that had smiled shyly earlier in the evening. She was pretty. Bright, glossy eyes looked at him with a hint of nervousness. There was a cigarette held between delicate fingers. Unlit.

Automatically Nathan began to pat his pockets, then felt foolish. Of course he didn't have a light.

"Sorry, I don't smoke."

The girl shrugged. "Never mind." The cigarette disappeared back inside its tattered packet. Then she leaned against the pillar close beside Nathan and looked towards the dance floor.

A hot ball of terror bounced through his insides. The tension returned with rapid, fiery breaths. He looked straight ahead. Oh shit, he thought. Oh shit oh shit oh shit. She was still there. She should have left. Why hasn't she left? He glanced towards her, she returned the glance and smiled. Nathan smiled back.

The girl straightened herself and moved closer. He could feel the heat of her body, and his own tingled in response as some of his reserve began to melt. Events moved of their own accord now. But that didn't ease the terror he felt; the fear of saying the wrong thing or making the wrong move.

"You're in here a lot," the girl said.

"Oh yeah. I like the place, you know. It's all right." Pathetic small talk. Nathan desperately tried to get his mind into gear. It wasn't easy. Show an interest, he thought, keep her talking. What did you say? When you got right down to it, what were you supposed to say? Richard would have known. Crude, shallow Richard would not have been lost for words.

"I've seen you around as well," he found himself saying. "I would have spoken to you before but I'm the shy type."

The girl smiled again and her eyes lit up. Evidently he had said something right. "I'm Lisa," she said.

"Nathan!"

This couldn't be happening. Adrenalin surged but his body was immobile, trapped between fight and flight. He wanted to run and hide. Equally he wanted to stay and talk. The twin urges cancelled out and dumped Nathan in the gulf of a sudden silence.

Lisa didn't seem to mind. She moved her body to the music and occasionally glanced at Nathan. He smiled back at her and sought for something to say.

"It's nice to have a bit of space, isn't it?" Lisa said after a while.

Nathan nodded, caught in the warm glow of her company.

"Bloody hell! She's a babe!"

Trouble was back. Nathan stiffened in horror and cursed under his breath. Why couldn't Richard leave him alone? Lisa didn't seem to notice and he struggled to recapture the gist of what she was saying.

"You're a dark horse," Richard said quietly. "You pulled her all by yourself? I'm impressed!"

"What was that?" He asked Lisa, leaning closer. He could feel Richard leering again, dreaded the suggestive comments that were assembling in his mind.

"Do you want to dance?"

"Me dance? I'm too drunk for that. I'd fall down!"

"He would too you know. Hopeless at dancing he is. Even when he's sober."

"That's all right," Lisa smiled. "I'm drunk as well - we can both fall down together."

"Bloody Hell Nathan what are you waiting for?"

Lisa took Nathan by the arm and began to drag him towards the dance floor. "Come on," she said and giggled. Nathan allowed himself to be pulled along. Richard followed.

"Ask her if she'd like some juicy red meat inside her!"

"NO!" Nathan screamed, spinning round. "Just go away, okay. Just get lost!"

"Nathan..."

"Just go away. Leave me alone. I've had enough!"

Lisa staggered backwards into the crowd. Nathan turned round just in time to see her disappear. Her confused face held a hint of pain and rejection. "Lisa. I didn't..." He began. But she was gone.

"You idiot!"

"Bastard! You just couldn't leave me alone. Could you? I was actually getting somewhere. Lisa actually liked me. And then you came along and ruined it."

"Wasn't me Nathan. You fucked it up all by yourself. Anyway, she wasn't your type."

"Just leave me alone!" Nathan stomped off, pushing people roughly out of the way. The bar beckoned.

Shadows danced before his eyes. Nathan wasn't sure if they were real or phantasms bred by alcohol. The images he perceived were grainy and unfocused, seen through a tunnel of darkness. The world sounded distant; noises just muffled thuds and tinny, high-pitched squeals that could have been voices. Only the double whisky in his hand was real. All else was illusion.

"Getting yourself drunk won't help," Richard said.

Nathan grunted incoherently.

"Plenty more fish in the sea."

Grunt.

"Just going to grunt all night are we?"

Nathan grunted.

"Okay Nathan. I'm sorry. I was jealous. That's why I got so nasty. Satisfied now? I've apologised. So are you going to snap out of it?"

Another grunt. The whisky slipped from Nathan's limp fingers and crashed to the floor.

Movement. His body was upright. A message left his chemical cocoon and somehow managed to get through. "Wha's h'pp'n'ng?" He slurred. He swayed a little before regaining sufficient control of his balance.

"I'm your friend Nathan - you can laugh - but I am," Richard said. "So I'm gonna help you get a woman. Okay?"

"There, she'll do," Richard said. Nathan didn't reply. He felt queasy and his head was spinning. Despite that he looked up and tried to focus on the girl in question. Vision failed to respond. The world seemed grainy, like a badly tuned black and white television.

"Get ready, Nathan, here comes the woman of your dreams!"

"Get off!" A woman's shrill voice pierced Nathan's stupor. It sounded distant and hollow in quality. Like it was coming from another room. A scream followed, then another.

Nathan felt himself thrown around. A wall - or something hard - slammed into his shoulder. Something else scratched his face. Another scream blasted through the dull humming in his ears.

"She's a goer this one!" Richard growled. "Come 'ere!"

The deep-buried, sober Nathan struggled to take control of his body. The chains of alcohol began to tear and Nathan fought to stop Richard.

"No!" He yelled as the girl pounded at Richard with her fists. He laughed and dragged her towards the toilets. Nathan struggled harder to fight back, aware of the horrified onlookers. Aware as their shock turned to angry action.

The girl was free. She ran off into the crowd, crying hysterically. Richard cursed. "Damn! The one that got away...."

An impact exploded in Nathan's face. He fell to the ground and something heavy landed on top of him. Hands roughly grabbed at him and suddenly he was yanked to his feet. Angry voices buzzed in his dazed mind.

"Where's Richard?" He heard himself cry. "Get Richard - it's all his fault!"

Down on his knees now. Somebody was standing over him and he pawed at their legs as his vision began to go dark. Then the cold floor touched his cheek and the world faded out.

Calm silence heralded the return of the world. Nathan lay in a null state between waking and sleep. Then he remembered flashing blue lights, men in uniforms and a hysterical girl.

"Oh God Richard! What have you done to me?" He wailed as the tears began to pour.

"Shut up you crybaby," Richard snarled. "I told you I could get a woman anytime I wanted. Well last night I wanted. So it's your fault we're in here."

"It's not my fault. How can you blame me? I didn't ask you to...."

"If you weren't such a useless lump of shit I wouldn't..... ach! Why did I have to get stuck with you?"

"But I didn't do anything!"

"No you never do. You whining little turd. You make me sick."

"Leave me alone!"

"That's so irritating. That's all you ever say. Well I'm not going to. It's your fault we're in here!"

Rage ignited in Nathan's heart. All he ever wanted was a little love and affection. Last night he nearly found it, only to lose it through Richard's cruel behaviour. He'd had enough of Richard, with his shallow, scornful ways and his insulting comments and aggressive manner. ENOUGH!

"Shut up! Just shut up. I'm sick of you, Richard. You hear me?"

Nathan unbuckled his belt, unfurled it from his jeans and wrapped it around his fist. Then he gripped the buckle and held the pin securely between two fingers.

"Nathan? What are you doing?"

The buckle flashed in the dull light as Nathan turned a menacing gaze on Richard. "I've told you to leave me alone!" He snarled.

The pin punctured flesh. Richard cried out. The pin struck repeatedly, shallow wounds multiplying to make a mass of torn and bloody flesh. Richard's screams grew fainter, until at last he fell silent. Still Nathan did not relent and hacked and stabbed with the pin. The only sounds now were his harsh breathing and the squelch of mutilated flesh.

Finally the pin, slick from Richard's blood, slipped from Nathan's grasp. The belt unwound and fell to the floor just as the cell door burst open. A man swore. Nathan giggled.

The cell was awash with blood. The two men followed Nathan's gaze down towards his stained and shredded crotch. Beneath the ripped material the mutilated organs gushed thick and red.

"He can't taunt me anymore," Nathan said, looking up at the ashen-faced men. "See - I shut him up forever!"

The Message

by
J T Howlett

James T Howlett

James. T. Howlett was born on August 22nd 1973. After showing a literary flair at school, he found himself forced to adopt a more realistic approach to life and started work as an electrical apprentice in 1989. He progressed through the ranks and is currently an electrical designer and estimator with a large mechanical and electrical firm in Suffolk. Having established himself in a good job, he re-approached his favoured subject of story writing with the intention of being published. He is currently working on a collection of short stories for his own book.

The Message

by

J T Howlett

It was a pleasant day at the beach, and a perfect one for the carnival to be in town. Seaside resorts were always popular in the Summer, and Arlen Bay was no exception. Crowds were everywhere - on the beach, pier and visiting the local shops, which all relied heavily on Summer trading to help them through the winter months. Arlen Bay was a Summer town - a bad Summer trade meant an even worse winter for its inhabitants.

This year though, things were booming largely due to the presence of the carnival - the first one to visit Arlen in 5 years. People were coming from all nearby places to visit the carnival.

One such person was 24 year old Paul Owen, who, somewhat reluctantly, had been persuaded to come by his 'girlfriend' Mary. Paul couldn't really refer to Mary as his 'girlfriend', she was more like a person who he wanted as a girlfriend but would probably have to settle for being friends. Paul was pretty certain Mary knew his intentions, but seemed happy just to leave it at that, but just when Paul had had enough she would interject a little comment into the conversation to keep Paul on tenterhooks. She seemed to do just enough to keep Paul hanging around, keep his hopes up, and it was gradually wearing Paul down. If she wasn't interested, why didn't she just say so?

So, as many times before, Paul agreed to come along, thinking this might be the time that something clicked: something happened between them.

They turned the street corner, faced with another pavement

sporting those shops that sell tacky shell ornaments, inflatable toys and gaudy postcards. The kind of stuff the inner city tourist delights at on their weekend away from the office.

"Hey, shall we go on the pier?" Asked Mary.

"Sure, why not?" said Paul, once again complying with Mary. Perhaps she would like it if he was more firm? She must like something to keep hanging around him, he reasoned.

The pier was old fashioned, its supports looking disturbingly fragile, and jutted out somewhere around 250ft into the sea. It was obviously totally safe by the size of the carnival on it, and it was the bright lights and loud music that had caught Mary's eye.

"£5.00 mate" a dishevelled youngster snapped at Paul from inside the confines of a grimy booth. Paul forgave him his rudeness, it must be damn boring sitting in that thing all day.

As Paul handed over the money, he glanced around to notice Mary already strolling inside. That was another thing - he always paid for everything. Mary was using him, why couldn't he just walk away and get on with his life? Sighing, he walked briskly to catch up with Mary, who was standing next to one of those driving arcade games, probably wondering how much change Paul had got.

"You ever had a go on this?" Mary said while accepting the £2 Paul had already removed from his pocket, and making herself comfortable in the driver's seat.

"No, I haven't. I'll let the expert show me how its done." Paul grinned as he watched Mary contort THAT body into the chair. His body reminded him that that was the reason he was still hanging around.

Mary placed the change into the machine, and selected the rugged mountain terrain as her racecourse. Paul hated driving games and was already bored at this early juncture. He looked around at what else was going on around him. There was a small rollercoaster, its main attraction being able to perform one 360 degree revolution in its confined quarters. Still, this was something special for most folk, as there was a good sized queue forming for it. Paul wondered how much that would cost him. Looking around further, the pier was dotted with those little stalls like the 'throw under 20 with 3 darts' and 'throw the hoop over the post' - were those things a con? Paul doubted that the hoop even fitted over the post. Perhaps winning a grotesque teddy for Mary would get him some brownie points. With the stalls in the middle, the perimeter of the pier was taken up with rides, mostly aimed at the younger generation, but then Paul guessed they would be. Despite being a kid at heart, Paul was deemed too old for that kind of thing anymore. Beyond all this, somehow people were managing to fish off the end of the pier, though Paul marvelled at their concentration, what with all the banality going on around them.

Paul had always been interested in horror and the more grue-some of things, clowns being a particular favourite. Clowns gave off an evil aura as far as Paul was concerned. He recalled a movie featuring Bumblebob the Clown, who used his friendly innocent appearance to conceal his murderous ways.

It was no surprise then, that Paul's eye was caught by the sight of a clown sitting in an old gothic style box, emblazoned with the caption 'Wheelie - the fortune telling clown 'and beneath this a further caption read 'for 50p he'll tell you what your future be'. Paul grimaced at the awful rhyme. However, the clown, Wheelie, was captivating. To the innocent eyes of a child, it was a symbol of fun, but to Paul the clown looked palpably evil.

Its grin seemed to mock him, the eyes daring him to ask his future. The eyebrows of the clown were furrowed very slightly, adding to the menace of Wheelie. How had this thing survived the age of computers and bright flashing things with funky noises Paul pondered.

A sharp prod knocked Paul out of his daydreaming.

"Have you got any more change?" Asked Mary.

Shit! Did she deliberately come out without money? Smiling, Paul said "Yeah, of course," and pulled out the sum total of his change. Sitting right at the top was a 50p piece, and Paul imme-diately glanced over at Wheelie, who was currently being ridiculed by 2 kids. Wheelie seemed to be taking it well.

Paul decided he wanted to take a closer look at Wheelie but didn't want to look too childish in front of Mary - things were going bad enough as it was. He reasoned that if they took a logi-cal route around the carnival, they should catch up with Wheelie on their way out.

They spent another 2 hours and £12 pounds of Paul's money indulging themselves in a Hall of Mirrors, various arcade machines (Mary), that tiny rollercoaster (the loop-the-loop made Paul feel ill) and a sort of miniature sea-world, which boasted an assortment of half dead livestock, which looked about 10 times as bored as Paul did.

Paul's interest did, however, pick up after emerging from 'the Undersea Kingdom', when he noticed that the only thing the carnival had left to offer was Wheelie.

Mary breezed past Wheelie without even a glance, and wasn't aware that Paul had stopped until she was near the exit, and the booth which contained the sullen teenager.

"Geez, what are you looking at thing for?" Questioned Mary.

Paul decided to pretend that he hadn't heard. He was enjoying a special moment with the clown.

Wheelie looked positively malignant to Paul. The painted eyes mocked him and what was meant as a friendly smile was transformed to an evil leer. The artist had done a really good paint job. The outside of the booth was not fairing so well; the dark green paintwork was peeling, and the coin slot was rusty. Paul wondered if the machine even accepted the new 50p piece.

"You're not serious are you?" Mary questioned once more, this time so close to Paul that he couldn't ignore her this time.

With a sigh Paul responded - "Why not? Perhaps I'll get some good news for a change," he rummaged around for 50p, and produced his remaining coinage. Mary huffed impatiently as he put the change in. Sod her, Paul thought; I'm doing something I want to do for a change.

The 50p went in easily enough, and the turnabout it produced in Wheelie was startling.

The clown became animated, lurching forward at Paul with what he considered to be evil intent. Accompanying the movement was a hideous laugh, which made Mary contort a face.

"He's charming isn't he?" Paul joked.

"Yeah a real nice guy." Mary replied and resumed looking bored. The laughter stopped, and a clicking noise made Paul look down. Out of a small hole, a little piece of paper protruded.

Paul peered at Wheelie, but the show was over, the clown had gone back to his normal position. Mary made a play for the paper but Paul intercepted her.

"Hey it's my future not yours," he said while thinking it could be yours as well.

"Knock yourself out," she said a little harshly.

Paul made a show of secretly looking at the paper, but was shocked at the message.

The small piece of paper simply said -

YOU WILL DIE - 12/05/98

Paul stared at it in disbelief. He looked back at Wheelie then back at the paper, but the inscription hadn't changed magically to something more pleasant. Noticing his expression, Mary said: "Not too good, huh? No millionaire status?"

Paul passed the message to her. Her eyebrows raised then furrowed as it sunk in.

"God, how morbid. That can't be normal can it?"

"Shouldn't think so. Perhaps the printer malfunctioned."

"Some malfunction." Mary had already discarded the paper and was moving off. Paul and his horrific imagination could not dismiss the incident so lightly. The message had unnerved him. Convinced it was a malfunction he was ready to try again. Upon checking his pockets, Paul was dismayed to find that he didn't have 50p. He would have to ask Mary. 50p was still a cheap day out.

"I want to have another go. Have you got 50p?" Paul asked Mary. Mary stopped, and, looking exasperated produced 50p from her jeans pocket. Raising her eyes to the heavens, she handed the money over and said:

"Here you go. What do you expect to happen?"

"I don't know. I can't believe that message was right. This is the only way to find out." He turned from her and approached

Wheelie once more. This time, instead of being fascinated by the clown, Paul found himself unable to look at it. The message really had unsettled him.

Hell, even his hands were sweating. He actually dropped the 50p which prompted Mary to snigger, and it was that that forced Paul to regain his composure. He retrieved the coin, and placed in the slot. The same performance ensued, but Paul kept his head bowed, nervously eyeing the hole where the message would emerge. The laughter pierced his sub-conscious daze, striking like a cobra at his nerves. The familiar click. The future had appeared in the hole. Trembling, Paul picked the paper up. The message read:

DEATH SHALL STRIKE YOU FROM ABOVE -
12/05/98

The dumfounded expression on Paul's face prompted Mary to enquire.

"What's it say? Come on, I'm dying to know." She giggled.

Paul handed her the paper. Her smile disappeared. "Shit. This is intense." She passed it back to Paul.

"This machine is seriously screwed up. What if a little kid read this? It can't be right." Said Paul.

"Perhaps it used to be one of those old spooky fate telling machines? You know, instead of the clown would be some spooky old crone predicting death for everyone? It's just a side-show machine Paul. Don't get all freaked out."

Don't get all freaked out. A machine had just told him he was going to die in 3 days time and that it would be "from above." What was there to get freaked out over?

Angry, he turned to Mary and said- "all right then, if this was one of those spooky old machines, how come it says 1998 on it? Surely it wouldn't predict death for someone in the forties as 1998. It might as well say you're going to die from old age."

"Hey don't get all snotty on me. I was just trying to offer an explanation. I don't know why it has done this and I don't really care."

Paul interjected, cutting her off. "It's not your death it has forecast is it?" He said sarcastically.

Changing the subject, Mary replied "can we go now?" Paul's logical side had started to reassert itself after losing control briefly to his imagination. His brain was already conjuring up logical explanations for the death messages. Printing error, some sicko at the factory slipping in some nice little predictions of his own.

"Yeah, OK., I suppose we should be going. We've both got work in the morning."

"Don't remind me," Mary groaned.

They started to make their way out. Other people were leaving as well, back to the city and the grindstone Paul thought. Another wasted day, only shortly livened up by a cranky old machine. Paul glanced back for a final look at Wheelie, when he noticed the clown being approached by a potential patron. A rather fat man in his early thirties was standing in front of the machine intently staring in. Paul stopped and watched as Fatty produced a 50p, and inserted it into the machine.

Nothing happened.

Fatty did not look amused, that 50p could buy food, Paul thought. Hey! His sense of humour was returning. Fatty, however, was not to be denied his prediction from Wheelie, as he grabbed a passing attendant. Meanwhile, Mary had noticed that Paul was gone. Turning around, she saw him looking at an obese man arguing with what appeared to be someone who worked for the carnival. She went back to Paul and enquired "What's going on?"

"That fat bloke put some money into the machine and nothing happened. I wanted to see what message he got." Paul said.

"Forget about it. Paul."

"I will, I just wanted to see what message he got, that's all."

What happened next gave both of them a chill down their spine.

Fatty had persuaded the agitated looking attendant to investigate why the machine swallowed his money without predicting his future. It didn't take him long. He peered down the back of the booth and emerged with the power lead and trailing plug in his hand. Wheelie hadn't been plugged in.

"Did you see that? Did you?" Mary looked at Paul. Paul was speechless. All he could do was stand and watch as the clown did his evil dance in front of Fatty (who looked less than impressed) and produce a small piece of paper. Mary was tugging at his sleeve, but Paul ignored her. Not for the first time today, a voice inside his head reminded him. Fatty picked up the paper, laughed, shook his head. Tossing it carelessly aside, he made a threatening look at a nearby hot-dog stall. He ambled off. It was all Paul could do to stop himself from bolting over and picking the paper up. Instead, he managed a calm stroll over to where Fatty had dropped the piece of paper. Mary stayed where she was. Bending down, Paul read the note.

YOUR FORTUNE LIES IN STOCKS AND SHARES, the message claimed.

By now Paul was really scared. He could not face the clown, but he could feel it watching him. He walked back over to Mary.

"Well? What did that one say?" She asked hurriedly.

"Same old shit. Our fat friend is going to die of a heart attack" Paul lied.

"See? I was right."

"How do you explain the plug then?"

"I can't really. Perhaps it was a build up of static, and the 50p released it. It was enough to trigger the machine off."

"Twice?" Paul countered.

"God, I don't know. You asked." Paul did ask, and he now decided to drop it. He would ponder over it later, he knew. They left the beach and carnival, and made their way back to the spot where Paul had left his car. It was still a nice day, the evening not cooling off much. People still wandered around in shirts and shorts, eating ice-creams. He longed to hold Mary's hand, but was scared of making the initial contact.

The drive home was rather subdued, Mary did not make much

conversation. Paul done all the work.

"So, doing anything exciting this week?" He enquired.

"No, nothing really," and so that was the pattern of the conversation until Paul pulled up outside Mary's flat at around 8.30pm. He dreaded these moments. He had been in this situation about 4 times now, the shall I put my arm over her attempt to kiss her scenario.

He had the most favourable of outcomes in his dreams, but in his dreams only.

They both sat there in silence for what seemed like an eternity, but was in fact a few seconds.

Summoning all of his courage, Paul half leaned over, looked squarely at Mary and said:

"Well, I've enjoyed today, what about you?" Shit! Real smooth Paul, he told himself. Hey, I'm building up to something, he retorted to the voice inside his head.

"Yeah, not bad." She shrugged non-commitally. Is this her way of saying back off, Paul wondered. If it was, it worked. Feeling his fragile self-confidence fragment and fall away like crushing a dead leaf in your hand and then opening it to the wind, Paul muttered:

"You've got my number if you need it. Maybe we can catch up with each other during the week?"

"Yeah, I'll give you a call" Mary let herself out of the car and walked to the stairs leading to her flat. Paul watched her disappear up the stairs, silently cursing himself. He had bottled it once again. What a wimp, Owen. He drove home, going over and over in his head what he should have said, what he should have done. But the moment was gone. Would he get the chance again? He did not know. If she didn't like him, why did she go out with him? Paul reasoned, trying to understand why they failed to make a connection. So many times before, he just couldn't get it. It was so damned frustrating. He gripped the steering wheel, hard, making his knuckles turn white with the effort.

The city buzzed at night, pubs and clubs pulling in people in their hundreds. As he drove past, Paul looked at them. Everyone seemed to have someone, except him. It just wasn't fair. But, as

Paul was quickly learning, life simply wasn't fair. It took every opportunity it got to give you a hefty punt in the lower abdominal area. A huge billboard caught Paul's eye, and he instantly wished it hadn't. The circus was coming to town (though god knows where they will pitch the big top), and the billboard was illustrated with a large picture of a smiling clown. The days events came flooding back into Paul's mind. How could he forget? He had been preoccupied thinking about Mary and had forgotten all about his run-in with the enigmatic Wheelie. He was going to die on Wednesday, the clown had predicted. This being the clown who should not have been able to work on the account of the fact he was not even plugged in. But he had worked. And told Paul he was going to die on Wednesday. Twice as well.

Paul was not superstitious, but couldn't help but feel that there was something in what happened to him. That machine had worked by itself for some reason or another, and despite Mary's technical explanation, Paul believed that it was to warn him of his death. He was being given another chance.

Bullshit, his sensible side told him. It was some prat at the factory, sticking his own message in with the others. You were just the poor sod who copped it, that's all. Stop worrying, and grow up. As he pulled up outside his house, Paul looked up warily to the sky. Death from above it had said. Paul had visions of a grand piano dropping on him like in the cartoons. Shaking his head at his own imagination, he unlocked his front door and stepped inside. The house was cold and empty, so Paul put the heating on. He sat down in the living room and picked up the t.v. guide to see if there was a decent late movie on. There wasn't, and so he decided to call it a day.

He trudged upstairs, downhearted in more ways than one, and entered his bedroom. As he removed his clothes, he fished around in his jeans pocket for the 2 messages. He still couldn't believe that they had really told him he was going to die. They weren't in his front right or left pockets, only a couple of receipts served as a reminder of where he had been today. They weren't in his back pockets either. Paul felt another surge of fear wash over him. He was sure he had pocketed the 2 messages, but they weren't here. He was sure. Thinking logically again, he argued with himself that he had simply thrown them away, like he should have done anyway. Discarded and forgotten about. This explanation was easier to accept than the other one for the machine working on its own.

As was his usual ritual, he removed his work clothes for the next day from his wardrobe, as he operated on auto pilot in the mornings. A new shirt, pressed trousers and shoes, an appropriate tie. He went to his wardrobe, retrieved his shirt and deftly avoided jolting the loose shelf above. One of the supports had broken, and the shelf leaned at an odd angle. He had meant to fix it ages ago, along with the broken tap and his back garden fence. He just never seemed to get around to these things, too much on his mind and tired from work all the time. He laid the items out on a chair and wearily climbed into bed. He picked up his latest bedtime reading, a paperback novel about giant insects plaguing New York city. A load of rubbish really, but easy reading just the same. After a few chapters, he felt his eyelids starting to struggle, so he put the book down, turned off his bedside lamp, and set his alarm clock. It was not long before he slipped into sleep.

He dreamed, and his dreams were dotted with images of fun-fairs and clowns, laughing and japing. He was wandering in an enormous carnival, people everywhere, bright lights and music assaulted his senses. "Want a balloon, sonny?" Paul turned around to see a clown leering over at him. "Uh, no thanks." Paul stammered, and backed off. The clown followed him, and Paul noticed others joining him. "Want a balloon sonny?" They all asked in unison. "Tell you your fortune sonny." they all said, and then burst out laughing as Paul turned tail and fled.

He raced past people, brushing them aside, and all the time clowns shouted at him as he run past, there were clowns every-where, the people he was brushing past were now clowns, he tripped, fell over, and a circle closed around him.....

Paul woke with a start, perspiration beading his forehead. This incident had pervaded his sub-conscious as well. He went into the bathroom, splashed water over his face and looked at himself in the mirror. He wasn't that bad looking, he had a good jaw line and straight roman style nose. His eyes were blue, and he had a healthy mop of brown hair. He pulled one of his eyelids down.

He didn't know why. He had just seen someone do it in a movie once. Sighing, he turned off the light and got back into bed. He slept peacefully for the rest of the night undisturbed and his sleep was only broken by his alarm clock at 7:30am. He woke feeling not that bad, considering his broken sleep. He showered, dressed and got in his car. He was on a tight schedule in the mornings, and rarely had time for breakfast. If he wanted breakfast, that would mean getting up earlier, and that meant less sleep. Yawning, he put the radio on and turned the key in the ignition.

The drive to work was uneventful, it often was at this time in the morning, and he pulled up in the firms car park and got out. He was usually the first one in, and Paul enjoyed the quietness of the office early in the mornings. He was an insurance clerk, not an interesting job, but one that paid the bills. He had worked with this firm all his life, from age 16, and now at 24 held a relatively senior position for one considered as still quite young. He looked at the papers on his desk. In a minute, he thought. Coffee first. He switched the machine on and waited for it to heat up. He made his coffee, sipped it and approached his desk and the mound of paperwork on it. He could genuinely say that he had had no thoughts on the events of yesterday. He hadn't forgotten them, they had simply been pushed to the back of his mind where they couldn't disturb him. He adjusted his calendar, and then instantly remembered. Was it just a joke? Or was he in serious danger? Paul just didn't know what to think. One thing was for sure though; he was going to be keeping it to himself. His work colleagues would have a field day with that one, he knew. It was the 10th May 1998.

There were 2 days to go.

The day's events at work were not exciting for Paul, but they did serve to make the day go quickly. He dictated 3 letters turning down insurance claims, fairly standard get-out clauses, and routine stuff. His firm was currently involved in some legal proceedings over repair work to one of their client's properties. He had missed a few premiums, and the firm were trying to use this as a way of getting out of paying. Well, most of it, anyway. Paul dictated 2 letters to this cause. He had a brief stint on the phone when covering for the girls at lunchtime and he had not realised what a nightmare tele-sales were until he did so. Whatever the girls got paid, it wasn't enough, he decided. The girls at the office were o.k., but not really his type. Mary was his type, but things were not working out there. But he could not afford the luxury of daydreaming at work, he needed to remain focused. He had a short, informal chat with his boss, who told him that if he contin-ued his 'sterling work' a senior management position at a nearby branch may be offered to him. "I think you're ready for it" his boss had said. He told his work-mates who were all pleased for him and it was agreed an after work drink was in order.

"Are you going to bring that bird you've been seeing then?" Nick said to Paul.

"No, I think we should keep it lads only, don't you?" This met with general approval, to Paul's relief. He did not want to get drawn into a discussion about that at the moment.

He finished work at 5:45pm and agreed to meet everyone in the pub (the first of many probably) at 8:00pm. He went home, prepared his usual meal of microwave crap, and sat down to eat it in front of the television. The news was the same old mish-mash of bad tidings and awful weather reports. No wonder he disap-peared into fantasy in his spare time. The world could be a mis-erable place sometimes. He sat through an episode of his favourite sit-com and then went upstairs to bathe. He had a good hot soak, letting the day's tensions drain out of him in the hot water. He closed his eyes.

Twenty minutes later, he emerged feeling refreshed and look-ing forward to a good night out on the town. Monday was nor-mally a quiet night, no women, but he had better things to cele-brate tonight, and for once, he wasn't worried about the opposite sex. He entered the pub at 8:05pm and his mates had already got a round in. The topic of conversation centred around the normal things, football and girls predominately. After a few more drinks, Paul was feeling pleasantly light headed, and in a better frame of mind than he had been in for days. They ended up going to a club, flirting a bit, and eventually calling it a night at around 1:00am. Paul called a taxi, said goodbye to his friends and headed home. He collapsed into bed and only just remembered to switch his alarm on before he dropped into the deep sleep of the drunken. He did not dream.

He awoke at the alarm's request, with a slight headache, but nothing that he couldn't handle.

He hadn't prepared his clothes, so he went to the wardrobe, and once again avoiding the shelf, removed his work attire.

And so this day at work was much the same as the previous one, and once more, it wasn't until he turned the leaf on his calendar that he was reminded of his impending 'doom'.

Death from above, the message had promised. Hmmm. He dismissed this thought from his mind as the first of his colleagues, Nick, came in.

"Hey Paul, really enjoyed last night. How are you feeling?" He enquired.

"My head is a little sore, but I'm fine." Paul answered.

"Yeah, know what you mean. I gotta lay off those whiskies. Why don't you guys stop me?"

"You looked like you were having a good time." Paul said with a grin.

"I was, that's the trouble." Nick laughed. Nick had a reputation for being able to "drink a bit" as he put it.

Paul made coffee for them both, and the day's work began.

It was the 11th of May 1998.

There was 1 day to go.

Paul and Nick went out for the hair of the dog at lunch time, and it actually seemed to improve Paul's condition. He wasn't sure he could say the same for Nick. It did, however, make him feel somewhat sleepy for the rest of the afternoon. The clock really seemed to be dragging its heels this afternoon (although Paul knew that was impossible).He noticed Nick taking frequent trips to the toilet and smiled to himself. Paul was out of the door at 5:00pm on the dot, (for once he didn't care what the boss thought) as there was a big football game on television tonight, and he wanted to get all of the housework done before it started.

He entered his house, checked for mail, there was none (no surprise there) and set about preparing his evening meal. No microwave trash tonight, he had a boil-in-the-bag special, beef madras curry. He filled a saucepan full of water and turned the ring on full blast to make the water boil. When the food was prepared, he sat down with the paper and began to eat. He managed about one mouthful before he lost his appetite totally.

The first thing he noticed on the paper was the date. It was the 11th, and that meant he died tomorrow. Well, according to Wheelie, that was. The now familiar feeling of dread crept over him, like a sheet coming to rest in the wind, laying on the ground. He made a decision right there and then. Last year at work, Paul only took 2 weeks holiday in an effort to show his commitment to his employers. This tactic had obviously worked, if he was to believe what his boss told him. Therefore, he had a total of 6 weeks holiday this year, so taking 1 day off shouldn't hurt, should it? Paul did not like giving in to his crazy, irrational side, but, if he didn't go outside and stayed indoors, he could not be harmed. So, for the sake of 1 day off, he could put all of this nonsense behind him, and get back to normal. (Whatever that was).

Paul began thinking. What illness could he fall foul of for one day? He settled in the end for the traditional upset stomach story, and hoped his boss did not make a note of it. Knowing he was going to be safe inside tomorrow, Paul felt more relaxed, and switched on the television to watch the match. At one moment, he picked up the paper to read his stars, but thought better of it in the end. That was his irrational side winning out again. He opted for the crossword instead. The match was sufficiently entertaining to take his mind off his 'problem'. Soon it was bedtime, and so Paul went to bed, read how the giant insects got killed, and finally to sleep. His dreams came out in force with no alcohol to subdue them, and he endured a painful rerun of the carnival dream. He did not wake this time however, but instead drifted into a more pleasant dream scenario involving him and Mary. Unfortunately, it is dreams like those that you do not want to end, and when they do, they have a pain all of their own.

Without his alarm clock to wake him, Paul came to at 8:15am and felt surprisingly relaxed seeing as this was his last day on earth. Boy, that dream was good, he thought, and as the dregs of it cleared, he looked beside him to confirm that Mary was not lying there. Rubbing his eyes, he felt a twinge of disappointment deep inside. Sighing, he got up and made his way into the shower. The hot jets of water pierced his mind and body, and washed away the dreams of the previous night. He could almost see them run down the drain, caught up in the water flow. If only all things could be washed away like that, Paul thought as he turned the shower off and groped blindly for his towel. He heard the paper drop through the letterbox downstairs, and the delivery boy moving off to his next call.

It was 12th May 1998.

There were no more days to go.

Whilst getting dressed, Paul had calculated that he was best off trying to time his call to work to get Nick. It would be easier talking to him than to any of the girls, or worse still, his boss. He decided around 8:40 would be a good time. He went downstairs, picked up the paper and studied the headlines. Boring. He looked at the back page for the sports headlines. More interesting. He went over to the telephone and dialled the firm's number. Bingo! Nick answered.

"Nick, its Paul. Look mate, I won't be in today. Got a bit of an upset stomach, you know? Can't venture any further than 5 yards from the bog."

"Oh I get you. Good night last night was it?" Nick laughed.

"No, no really its true. I did have a curry though." That ought to do it, Paul thought.

"Yeah, right. Those things can be bad news sometimes. OK., I'll tell old stoneyfeatures for you. See you tomorrow, yeah?"

"Yes, sure, its one of those 24 hour things I think. See ya."

"Bye" Nick hung up. Paul sighed. This kind of thing was not in his nature. He went into the kitchen, which looked surprisingly neat for a single man. Paul believed in cleanliness, especially in the kitchen where food was prepared. He made a cup of tea for himself, and sat down in the living room to study the paper. After reading about gay nazi vicars in sex storms and the like, he went over to the window to see what kind of day he was going to be missing. Gazing out, it didn't look like the kind of day in which he could be killed. Then what kind of weather did he expect? Dark skies with flashes of lightning and rumbles of thunder like an old Hammer Horror film? He looked across the street and gasped. His jaw dropped open in disbelief at what he was seeing.

Across the street, and staring straight back at him was none other than Fatty. The same Fatty from the carnival. The same Fatty who also visited Wheelie, but fared somewhat better. Paul jumped away from the window, but it was too late. Fatty had seen him, and started to walk over. Paul hid in the hallway, and stared at the frosted window in his front door. Nothing. And then a huge shadow fell over it, blocking out nearly all of the light. Paul's heart was screaming like a demented banshee. He put his hand on his chest. The doorbell rang. Once. Twice.

Struggling to regain composure, Paul walked over to the door. Assuring himself that his safety chain was latched, he opened the door. The chain only allowed about 3 inches for the door to open, but that was enough.

Fatty was even larger close up. He had a smallish head, balding, Paul noticed. He was wearing a Timberland T-shirt, which was clearly struggling to contain his bulk. Completing the outfit was a pair of jeans and walking boots. In his right hand he fiercely clutched a king-size Mars bar.

"Er, yes?" Paul enquired as politely as he could.

"All right mate? I'm looking for Agate Close and I think I've fucked up somewhere. Do you know where it is?" Fatty demanded. Paul felt so relieved that this fat man wasn't going to kill him that he started laughing. Death from above? Well, he certainly was taller than Paul.

He laughed uncontrollably. Fatty looked totally perplexed. Paul was giggling like a small child at something rude or dirty. Fatty stepped back, bemused. Paul did not notice. "weird bastard" he mumbled to himself, and went off in search of someone more useful. Like an old lady, who maybe even had the kettle on.

Paul finally gained control of himself, and noticed that Fatty had gone. He felt a pang of guilt. The poor sod was lost, and Paul did not help in. Instead, he let his wild imagination go running off again. Feeling bad, he unlatched the door and stuck his head outside to see if he could still help Fatty, if he was still around. Looking up the street he saw nothing. Looking down the street, he saw Fatty chatting to an elderly lady, who was making dramatic gestures with her hands. Obviously giving directions, Paul thought.

With sudden crystal clear clarity, Paul realised that he was outside. Well, his head was anyway. He jerked himself back indoors, and replaced the latch on the door. He went back into the living room and once more looked out the window. No huge object was embedded in the pavement where he had been peering out. That could have been it, Paul thought. Grow up, he scolded himself. He needed another cup of tea to calm him down. God, not even 1/3rd through the day, and already he was a bag of nerves. He ignored the kitchen and opted for a shot of brandy instead. That should calm him down more. He gulped the brandy, feeling its warmth slowly spread through his insides. That was much better. He finished his drink and put the tumbler down. He looked at the bottle. It was a new bottle he had opened, and judging by the way it had gone down, Paul had just had nearly a tumbler full. He hadn't realised. I must be really unnerved, Paul concluded.

He spent over an hour fixing the busted tap in the kitchen, an awkward job not helped by the fact that Paul banged his head under the sink. Quite hard too, judging by the bump that was now beginning to form. He was duly rewarded though when he turned the tap on and water came out for the first time in months. Smiling, he turned it off, pleased with the results of his impromptu d.i.y. work. He was considering tackling the upstairs wardrobe shelf with his new surge of confidence when something made his mind stop dead in its tracks.

The doorbell had rung again.

Once more, Paul gazed uncertainly at the door, and again, there was a dark shadow that he could make out through the frosted glass. The doorbell rang again, nagging at his mind, telling it that it would not go away. Sweat popped out on his forehead.

Adopting the same procedure as before (well it had worked

hadn't it?) he ensured the latch was firmly in place, and opened the door, standing a little back as well, for extra safety. Through the constricted opening, Paul could make out two men, dressed in casual work clothes. One appeared to be on the run from the fashion police and the other looked somewhat more presentable. Both of them were in their mid-thirties. Paul noticed a works van mounted on the pavement outside his house. He could not make out the writing on it due to his restricted viewing area. Both men displayed Council identification badges, identifying the badly dressed man as Bob and the other guy as Greg. They didn't wait for Paul to speak.

"Hello mate. We're filling in a small hole in the road out there and was hoping you could make us a cup of tea." Greg said. They looked at Paul hopefully.

You cheeky sods Paul thought. However, they had obviously done this several times, and Paul admired their gall. "Yeah sure," he smiled. "How do you take it?"

"Pretty weak no sugar." Said Bob.

"Pretty strong 1 sugar" said Greg. Hmmmm, thought Paul. It wasn't just dressing style they differed in either. He left the latch on the door and went into the kitchen. Outside, a drill had been started up. They didn't hang around. Five minutes later he emerged with two mugs of hot tea in his hands. He unlatched the door, and called out. Neither of the two men could hear Paul over the noise of the drill, and they had their backs to him. He had two choices; leave the tea on the doorstep, where it might get left for ages and go cold before they got to it, or, go over and take it to them. So he strolled outside carrying the tea, not thinking twice. He could feel the vibrations of the drill under his feet. As he got nearer, the drilling stopped and both men turned round to face Paul. It was as if they had heard him coming, Paul thought. He handed over the mugs.

"Cheers mate." They both said in uncanny unison. Another well rehearsed line. Delayed reaction struck Paul again, and he realised with horror that this time, he was standing outside, a good 8 yards from his door. Totally exposed. He suddenly felt like he was the only visible object for miles around on a flat land-scape. Not thinking or caring what it looked like, Paul bolted for his front door. He nearly made it, too.

Just as he was about to set his right foot inside his doorway, he tripped on the doorstep, and fell inside, landing in an untidy heap in the hallway. His foot hurt from where he caught it.

He picked himself up, cursing himself for losing it once more, now that he was safe inside.

All of this had been observed both of the workers and Bob shouted out "You all right mate? Something wrong?"

"Er, the phone was ringing." Quick thinking, Paul. He took the opportunity to shut the door.

"I couldn't hear a phone could you Greg?" Said Bob.

"No, but that bloke doesn't look right does he? Probably on drugs or something."

"Yeah, probably." Both men laughed and went back to work.

Inside the house, Paul had once more turned to the brandy bottle to calm his frayed nerves.

He did not bother with a glass this time, he just drunk it straight from the bottle. At this rate, he would be drunk by teatime. The brandy took longer to work this time, but still ended up having the desired effect. By 12:30pm, the roadworks were completed, and Paul observed the two men loading the van up. Greg picked up the two mugs and walked towards Paul's front door. Inevitably, the doorbell rang, but Paul had already made his mind up that he would not be answering it. As if sensing this, Greg did not really hang around. He left the mugs on the doorstep and got in the van. The engine started, and the van moved away. Paul felt some of his anxiety drive off with them.

Getting through this day was proving to be harder than he thought. He had expected some anxious moments, but had been in near panic twice now.

Paul decided he needed something to occupy his mind. He went upstairs, and selected two of his favourite films to pass the time away. He left the Killer clowns on the shelf, and opted for two low budget horror flicks, something to provide some light relief. As he reached the living room, his clock struck 1:00pm, and Paul's stomach came to life right on cue. He made for the kitchen.

Paul had not been prepared for his sudden day off, and the contents of his cupboards reflected this. Nothing, really. A few bags of crisps, a tin of beans and a few slices of bread. Beans on toast it was then.

He ate the meal in the kitchen, washed it down with some milk, and went back into the living room. He switched the television and video on and stuck the first tape in. He found himself wondering what had been going on at work, and again felt a twinge of guilt for the way he had deceived his boss and friends. Well, soon he could put it all behind him.

He settled back on the sofa and watched the movie.

He reached down and removed the second tape from the machine. As he reset the video, the time flashed up at him. Heck! It was 5:27pm. He had wasted the whole afternoon. Or rather, lasted the whole afternoon. He was two thirds through the day, he had almost made it!

Paul was snapped out of his euphoria by the ringing of the telephone. Now what?

He went over to it and picked up the receiver. "Hello?" He said tentatively.

"Hello, is that Paul?" A female voice enquired. Mary's voice. The hair on Paul's neck stood on end at the sound of her voice. He tried to sound calm, assured.

"Hi Mary. How's it going?"

"Oh, fine yourself?" Another sparkling conversation thought Paul dryly.

"I'm fine, just fine." He lied. Attempting to call her bluff he said: "So what can I do for you Mary?" Her answer dumfounded him.

"I was wondering if I could come round tonight. I've rented that new horror film you wanted to see on video, and thought we could watch it together."

So, this was it then, Paul thought. He could hardly believe it. There was no film on video he wanted to see, they both knew that. His heart pounding, Paul could barely get the words out.

"Yeah. Yeah sure. Why not?" He stammered.

"Great, I'll see you around seven then. Bye." She hung up.

"Bye." Paul said to the dead receiver and then cradled it. Reality bit in - seven! In that time he had to have tea, have a shower, put on some decent clothes, tidy the house up....

Thank god for his sensible side. Mary was permanently hungry; he reasoned therefore that he could order some food in when she was here; that left him more than an hour and a quarter to run the cleaner round, take a shower and smarten himself up.

He performed his cleaning duties first, with more gusto than he had ever shown before. His mind was working overtime thinking of what may happen that night. He put the cleaner away and bounded up the stairs to the bathroom. He jumped in the shower and did not come out until he was sure that he was thoroughly cleansed. He was taking no chances. He went to his wardrobe and found that his desired shirt needed ironing. No problem, thought Paul.

He erected the ironing board, and went back to the wardrobe for the shirt. He removed it via the hanger, which snagged on the rail. He yanked it free, and it was this force that caused the shelf above to give up its already precarious grip on stability. It came crashing down, spilling its contents onto the floor, and over Paul. The more notable of these contents was the iron itself. The pointed end of the iron struck Paul firmly on the side of the head, knocking him flat on his back. His consciousness flailing, the room spinning, Paul groaned and managed to roll over. Then darkness. Nothing.

He opened his eyes. His head hurt. Rubbing where he guessed the sore spot to be, Paul looked around his room. The memory of what happened came flooding back. No brain damage then. It was 6:55. Mary! He sat up, still rubbing his head. A large bump was forming.

He went into the bathroom to inspect the damage. He was cut, but not too badly. He placed a plaster over the wound, wincing as he pressed it down. It made him look really attractive.

He re-entered his bedroom and put back the mess the best way he could. The doorbell rang. She was here. The shirt would have to wait. He found he had to take it easy down the stairs; maybe he had a little concussion. Hospital would have to wait though. He opened the door, and there was Mary, looking more beautiful than ever before. She had gone to some lengths with her appearance tonight. He ushered her into the house, and closed the door behind him with a grin on his face. "You hungry?" Asked Paul.

"Yeah, I am actually. Got anything to eat?"

"I thought maybe we could order something in." Said Paul. "How about Indian?"

"Sounds great."

Paul placed an order on the telephone and then joined Mary in the living room. She had already made herself comfortable on the sofa. He was getting some strong vibes off her.

"Shall we wait for the food before we put the video on?" He said.

"Good idea. Come and join me over here." She motioned for him to sit on the sofa. He did so. "What have you done to your head?" She asked, noticing the plaster there.

"Got a little bump on the head is all." Paul shrugged. She leaned over and tenderly touched the wound. Paul flinched, but not really from the pain. An electric charge was building up between them, and they both leaned toward each other. They shared a passionate kiss. Paul genuinely thought he was dreaming.

When at last they parted, Mary said "Feel any better?"

"Much," was all Paul could manage as a reply. He simply could not believe that this was happening to him. They sat facing each other, matching each other's gaze. Their reverie was broken by the doorbell. Their food had arrived. Reluctantly, he got up from the sofa. When he reappeared, Mary was busying herself in the kitchen. She seemed to know where everything was. The evening turned out to be nothing short of perfect. Paul opened a bottle of wine to go with their meal. Whilst watching the video, Mary laid on Paul on the sofa, cuddling up to him when a scary moment happened. Paul knew she was not scared.

With only the television screen to illuminate his face, he smiled to himself. What had gotten into her? Who cares? Another voice asked. This is what you wanted isn't it? Yes, Paul agreed, this is what he wanted. He put his arm round her and watched the film. When the movie was finished, Paul got up and started to clear the dishes away. Mary took his hand and said "Those can wait can't they?" She had a devilish look in her eye that Paul had not seen before.

They went upstairs.

Paul was abruptly woken by the alarm clock. Another dream. He touched his head and winced at the sharp bolt of pain he received when doing so. The cut was real. He looked beside him and saw Mary looking back at him.

"Good morning lover." She smiled at him.

Lover. Lover. She had called him lover. He bent over and kissed her and last night had been no dream at all. Their love-making was sweet reality. There was also something else; but at present he could not put his finger on it. They both got out of bed and got dressed. Paul for work; Mary in what she had been wearing last night.

"Can I give you a lift home?" Said Paul.

"No, it's fine thanks. No work for me today. I'll enjoy the fresh air. Hadn't you better get moving though?"

Paul realised that he was running late. They made their way downstairs, and nearing the door, Paul stooped down to pick up the paper. So that was it. He felt as if a huge weight was lifted off his shoulders when he saw the date. The thirteenth May. He had survived. Mary had helped him forget the horror of yesterday and he had eventually sailed through his supposed last day on earth.

He stepped outside, Mary beside him, and they kissed before they parted.

"When.." Paul began.

"Tonight." Mary interrupted. They both grinned at each other, Mary with that same wicked grin of the previous night. She walked off up the road.

Paul got into his car with the first genuine smile he had worn on his face in over 6 months. Just as everything had seemed to be going wrong, everything was now going fine. Just fine.

Wrong, wrong and wrong. What Paul had failed to realise (and to be fair a lot of other people wouldn't have thought of this) was that Wheelie the fortune telling clown was of American origin. Accordingly, he was manufactured, built and assembled in America. That included the fortune messages.

Whatever force, good or bad, that had used Wheelie that day had not got it wrong. It had simply communicated to Paul through the machine, an American machine. It was as precise as a surgeons scalpel in its prediction of 12/05/98.

Extract from the local evening newspaper 5th December 1998.

MAN KILLED IN TRAGIC ACCIDENT

A young man was killed tragically today when he was struck by a golf ball whilst walking across Arlen City golf course. The course, which is also commoner's land has never had a reported incident like this before in its 12 year history. A sad statistic to have to add.

Paul Owen, 24, was killed instantly by the golf ball. He was believed to be walking at the foot of a big slope on the 12th hole. The accident happened at around 12.30pm. He was found by the 2 golfers who were playing that hole. Mr Owen's fiancee, Mary Brightman, was said to be 'devastated'. The couple were planning to wed in April.

©J T Howlett

The Driver

by
Nick Daws

Nick Daws

Nick Daws is a professional freelance writer. He was born in Carshalton, Surrey forty-two years ago. A psychology graduate from Leicester University, his early career included a range of jobs in education and the voluntary sector. He has been a full-time freelance for the last eight years.

Nick is the author of seven non-fiction books, three correspondence courses and the multimedia tutorials CREATIVE WRITING and SHORT STORY ACUMEN (Way Ahead Electronic Publishing). He lives in Burntwood, Staffordshire, with his partner Jayne, an IT specialist with a large building company, and a variable number of cats.

The Driver

by

Nick Daws

It would not be true to say that I enjoy driving - in my circumstances, that would indeed be an irony - but if ever I can achieve a certain equanimity it is at this time of night, three in the morning, when the roads are slick and dark and all but deserted. At these times I relax and let the car look after itself, just one hand on the steering wheel as we scream and slide round every bend. Perhaps you've seen me, if ever you drive on ill-lit country roads late at night. I've imagined you cursing as I passed you on the corner, and I've laughed to think how little meaning your curses can have for me.

Petty this may be, but it fills the time, and filling time is my greatest challenge. I listen to the radio a lot. Not the big national stations, which I find dull and ponderous, devoted to the discussion of world affairs which no longer have any bearing on me - but the locals, with their community news, their home-spun DJs, their cosy phone- in programmes. I have become quite an expert on wavebands and frequencies. I spin the dial as I travel, following the stations from Piccadilly to Mercia, Wyvern to Severn Sound. I listen to them fade slowly away, and welcome them back like old friends as I re-enter their transmission areas.

The radio is to my left, just below the dashboard. By contrast with the car, which is small and functional, the radio is a luxury model. It has three wavebands, volume and tone controls, a tuning dial and six presets. The last appear to have been tuned to distant European stations. They rise and fall through the night, fading to static with the dawn. In front of me is a round speedometer marked in gradations of 10 mph up to a maximum of 120. Other instruments include a small ammeter marked simply '+' and '-', a fuel gauge and a stalk bearing the lighting controls and indicators. These are my constant companions.

It is a wet and blustery October night. Rain buckets against the windscreen. The wipers are going at full speed, but still the landscape distorts behind a film of water. There are few other cars on the road and not a pedestrian in sight. Thunder rolls behind me, and a bolt of lightning forks to earth a short distance across the fields. In the electric flash I see her, a girl by the roadside, about eighteen, wearing a knee-length duffel coat and tightly - coiled scarf. Her blonde hair is long, wind matted and rain soaked. She raises a thumb at me hopefully. The thunder cracks and booms. It is no night for hitchhikers, no night especially for such a young girl. I squeeze the brake pedal, slide to a halt about fifty yards past. I watch her, half walking, half running, in my wing mirror. I turn off the late show and roll down the window. The rain lashes my face.

"Where are you going?"

"Oxford. Are you - ?"

I feel a sudden twinge. "Jump in," I say.

"Thanks."

I reach over, open the passenger door. I keep a smile on my face to hide the pain. She walks round, climbs in. She sits, leans back as I reach over and slam the door. The pain begins to diminish.

"What a night," she says.

"Yes," I reply. My voice sounds odd to my own ear, lacking inflection.

"Last time I go to a party with..." The name is mumbled and I don't catch it. The girl takes a pocket mirror from her small handbag and peers at her face in it. Finding a loose strand of hair, she pastes it back behind her left ear. "Sorry about your car."

"What?"

She looks at me. "Dripping. On your upholstery." She drops the mirror back in the handbag, clicks it shut. "Uh, are we going then?"

"Yes. Sorry." I release the handbrake and pull away. From the corner of my eye I can see her watching me.

"Are you OK? You look tired."

"I'm all right. Been driving a while."

"You look it."

I stare at the road ahead. This section curves gently away to the left. We are nearing Long Compton, and the ancient Rollright Stones are a mile or so on the right somewhere. I see another car approaching round the next bend and dip my lights. The car appears, headlamps dazzling me for a moment, then passes by.

The girl is looking at the dashboard. Perhaps she is puzzled by the lack of identifying marks. "What kind of car is this?" She asks.

"I don't know," I say.

I see her studying me.

"Isn't it your car then?"

My car? My coffin, more like. Of course I cannot tell her this, but possibly she sees the faint, ironic smile that crosses my face.

"Hey. You're not some kind of weirdo, are you?"

I start to speak, but she interrupts.

"I'd better warn you, I've done classes in karate."

"I'm not a weirdo," I say. "I'm just tired. And I don't know what make the car is. I think it's from Eastern Europe. I'm borrowing it from a friend."

She seems satisfied with this, for she leans back, and looks out at the night-time panorama. There is not much to see - just hedges, fields, trees, and the occasional building, shadowed and mute.

"You can drop me off in the middle of Oxford," she says. "If that's convenient."

I nod, and she lapses into silence again. I allow my thoughts to drift sidewards.

I don't remember much of what came before. I believe I had a wife, a job, children. But thinking about it now is like trying to remember an old black-and-white film seen on television ages ago. A late film, viewed through a haze of alcohol and ennui. Much of what I recall is bland, innocuous. But there are also darker moments. These I would rather not describe. Whether they are nightmare, fantasy, slivers of the truth, I do not know.

The only thing I can believe about my past is that I have spent what already seems an eternity driving this car. I cannot explain it except in Old Testament terms - that I have been judged and condemned for some transgression I do not remember, and this is my punishment.

Next to me my passenger is silent. She stares, apparently unconcerned, through the window - but I note that her fists are clenched, the knuckles white. I feel an urge to say something, anything, to break the silence.

"Are you a student?"

"That's right." She seems relieved to speak. She turns to me, smiles. "I'm at Exeter College. Do you know it?"

"Yes. What are you studying?"

She hesitates, and I notice her biting her lip. I suppose I was too abrupt. I am out of practice at making small talk. After a moment she continues brightly.

"I'm reading History, Ancient and Modern. Quite appropriate, really. In Oxford, I mean."

I nod, thinking about history. "Do you know anything about mythology?" I ask.

"A bit." She smiles nervously. "Greek, Roman, Norse - take your pick."

"How about the Flying Dutchman? Do you know that one?"

"The Flying Dutchman? Funny you should ask. I was reading up on it recently." She has become animated now, perhaps on the assumption that while we are conversing I am unlikely to commit some atrocity. "The story's told in different ways. According to one version, the Flying Dutchman was originally a vessel laden with precious metal. But one day a murder was committed and plague broke out among the crew. No port would allow the ship to land, and it's said she still travels the oceans, doomed to be sea - tossed, never to enjoy rest."

I nod. She takes a deep breath, continues: "Wagner told it differently in his opera. According to him, the captain brought doom upon his ship when he swore to get round Cape Horn 'if he had to fight God and the Devil till Doomsday'. Take your pick, as I say."

Is that me, I wonder. Doomed to pilot this car forever for committing some dreadful crime? Or perhaps the myth of Prometheus is more appropriate. My passenger is staring through the window again, so this time I fill in the details myself. Prometheus stole fire from Olympus and gave it to mankind. For his presumption Zeus chained him to a rock with a vulture pecking at his liver. Being immortal he couldn't die, but he suffered terrible pain. And so it went on, till at last Hercules released him by slaying the vulture.

Could that be me? Being punished not for a crime but some noble, if misguided, act? I'd prefer to believe that. I don't feel as though I'm a criminal. But I'd like to know - who will rescue me from this fate?

Or perhaps the answer does not lie in mythology at all. Perhaps my being here is no more than a glitch, a bug in the cosmic programme. In which case, where do I appeal to have things set right? Will anyone help me? Does anyone know I exist?

By now we are travelling into Oxford. Bright lights line the road on both sides, illuminating shop windows. I drive down the High Street, past the Town Hall and into St Aldates. "Could you drop me off along here?" my passenger asks. I bring the car to a halt beside a women's boutique. A blue neon sign flashes in the window: EXPERIENCE, it says.

The girl smiles tentatively. "Well, thanks for the lift..." She opens the door.

I have to tell her! I must!

"Please," I say, ignoring the warning stab.

"Yes?" She says, non-committal. She glances along the street, perhaps measuring the distance to safety.

"I'm...prisoner..." A torch ignites inside me. I close my eyes, try to stop myself shaking.

"What's the matter? Are you ill?"

How can I make her understand?

"Can't...leave..."

"Who says?" She opens the door again, the muscles in her body tensed. I have only a split second or she will flee. What can I say to keep her here? I force my mind to function, try a line she herself suggested.

"I'm...ill." I slump back in my seat. The groan I emit is spontaneous.

She sighs, very softly, and allows the door to close again. I see her glance longingly down the street. Then she turns to me.

"What's the matter?" She asks.

"It's a...mental...condition..." The pain is coming in waves now, in time with the flashing sign outside.

"What are the symptoms?"

"I can't...leave...car."

"Uh..." She looks puzzled for a moment. "Like agoraphobia?"

"Like that...yes."

"That's why you were asking about the Flying Dutchman?" She laughs nervously.

"Yes!" I reach out and grab her wrist. This is a mistake. I feel as though I have grabbed a live cable. Agony surges through me, and the world fades to black.

When I open my eyes again she is still there, fear and concern mingling in her face. I see her relief I am still alive. I am not sure she is right in this conclusion, but in any case I wish I could share the sentiment.

"Can you drive a short way? The Infirmary's back there. I think they have a Casualty - "

"Don't...leave me..." Our eyes meet. She shakes her head in momentary confusion.

"I'm sorry. I - I've gotta go." She opens the door and takes a couple of backward steps: "Woodstock Road - follow the signs." She turns and breaks into a run. I hear her feet pounding the wet pavement. It occurs to me I never asked her name.

And all is silent. The sign in the window mocks me. The pain is a steady state, unbearable, yet for a short while I am able to ignore it, locked as I am in a cage of my own grief.

Then I close the door, put the car into gear, and accelerate away.

©Nick Daws

Look out for other titles in the

CLOVERBOOKS

series of short story anthologies

SPIRIT OF DARKNESS II
SUMMER LOVING
CHRISTMAS SPIRIT